PLANET OF NO RETURN

By
HOWARD BROWNE

ARMCHAIR FICTION
PO Box 4369, Medford, Oregon   97501-0168

RESCUE MISSION TO AN UNTAMED PLANET

The Princess Ana-Bet came millions of miles across space and faced the terrors of an untamed planet in search of her missing lover. But once finding herself caught in the searing gaze of a lustful savage she wondered…could this be what she was really looking for?

In addition to being an action-filled science fiction thriller, Howard Browne's "Planet of No Return" is an epic interplanetary love story that transcends not only the lines of social propriety, but the laws of the universe. Join the courageous crew from Andara and the intrepid inhabitants of a barbarian planet as man and woman, civilized and uncivilized, collide in a hectic fight for freedom, love, and glory.

FOR A COMPLETE SECOND NOVEL, TURN TO PAGE 101

CAST OF CHARACTERS

HAD-SUDOL
Captured by a savage and barbarian race, this man had no hopes of returning home, nor was he sure he wanted to.

ANA-BET
This impetuous, spoiled princess of Andara really had some clout—until a savage barbarian her got her in his grip!

VALAR
A valiant noble caveman of the Polex tribe. He was the greatest hunter of his kind. And whatever he wanted and got…he kept.

DULEEN
An unusual blonde-haired beauty, her passion and self-assured ways were not to be ignored.

RHON-DEE
As Commander of the rescue fleet in service to Princess Ana-Bet, his patience—and his heart—were bound to be tested.

GLAT-STEVO
He was the Captain of the fleet and would put his life on the line for his Commander, his country, and his Princess.

ULGO
Tribal elder of the barbarians that imprisoned Had-Sudol, his tribe's welfare, and his ego, were his biggest concerns.

CHAPTER ONE

THEY came down out of a hot blue sky late one afternoon some twenty thousand years before the birth of Christ of Galilee. There were seven of them: long sleek metallic projectiles that gleamed like frosted silver in the golden sunlight.

The seven settled to earth in smooth silence, to form a long uneven line, one behind the other, among the lush grasses of a wide valley flanked by towering cliffs. For some time there was no other movement, no sign of life around those silvery hulls, while, within, technicians made tests of the unknown planet's atmosphere and studied the rolling semi-tropical terrain through powerful instruments.

In the flagship an audio-screen set in one wall of a luxuriously appointed cabin glowed with sudden light and a muted bell sounded a single note. Rhon-Dee, commander of the space fleet, leaned his lean and muscular body back in his chair and lifted cold blue eyes to the face of an under-officer framed in the square of frosted glass.

"Well?" the commander said quietly.

The face in the screen was impassive. "Atmosphere: oxygen twenty percent, nitrogen seventy-nine percent, remaining one percent consists of argon, neon and traces of two unidentified gases—both harmless. Atmospheric pressure: slightly under fifteen pounds to the square inch."

The commander's nod was barely perceptible. "Signs of life?"

"Numerous small, winged creatures. Several groups of small arboreal animals not yet identified. A herd of herbivorous animals, four-footed, about the size of *zilots*. No indication of any higher forms of life."

Commander Rhon-Dee's expression gave no clue to his thoughts. He looked slowly down at the charts and astral maps stacked neatly on the dull green metal of his desk top, and it was almost a full minute before he spoke again.

"Form a reconnoitering party—twenty men, heavily armed—and await further instructions. Have Captain Glat-Stevo come to my cabin immediately."

"At once, Commander."

The screen darkened and Rhon-Dee reached for the logbook and with a stylus entered several cramped notations on a fresh page. As he finished, a rhythmic knock sounded at the door and a tall broad shouldered young man in uniform entered, saluted briskly and swept the cabin with a single glance.

"Close the door, Stevo," Rhon-Dee said mildly, using the diminutive of the other's name, as was customary among close friends.

Glat-Stevo banged the portal shut with a thrust of his foot, dropped into a chair across from the commander and swung the heels of his polished boots to rest on one corner of the desk.

FOR A LONG moment the two men sat there without speaking, each well aware of what the other was thinking. Both were case-hardened fighting men, veterans of numerous campaigns on their home planet. They had graduated, as classmates, with highest honors from their country's war college, and the air arm of Andara's armed forces was their immediate choice. In a world constantly torn by wars, the two close friends rose rapidly through the ranks to high commissions. It was Rhon-Dee's bent for organization, plus a touch of caution completely lacking in his friend, that had put him slightly higher up the scale than Glat-Stevo; but there was no envy or jealousy in the latter's entire makeup and the difference in rank imparted no strain on their relationship.

"Well, we made it," Glat-Stevo said cheerfully and unnecessarily.

Rhon-Dee, idly turning the stylus between his powerful fingers, only grunted.

"Which means," Glat-Stevo continued, still cheerfully, "that Had-Sudol probably made it too."

"Not at all," Rhon-Dee said sharply. "Had-Sudol started on his insane journey more than three years ago. Instruments and fuel needed for interplanetary travel were hardly beyond the experimental stage in those days."

"So it would have required six months instead of three," his companion said. "And a landing here might have been somewhat more perilous. But this planet was his target and the chances are excellent that he hit it—and all your wishful thinking to the contrary is wasted."

"Then," the commander snapped, "why did he fail to return?"

"That is what the Princess Ana-Bet wants to know— and the reason seven space ships and five hundred of Andara's best warriors have traveled something like 43,000,000 miles. Love is a powerful emotion, my friend; I must try it sometime!"

"In this case," Rhon-Dee said, "it is outright madness. With what this expedition has cost our country an entire army could have been outfitted and placed in the field. Our borders are ringed with enemies who may strike at any moment; yet here we are, far from home, on a fool's errand. There was no reason why it could not have been postponed another year, when conditions might be less explosive."

Glat-Stevo's smile was wry. "Conditions are always explosive on our world. Which is why, even with the equipment for space travel in our hands, we have never before made the attempt. Another year—another ten years!—and there would still be wars about to begin, or about to end so that they might begin again. So who shall blame the Princess for refusing to wait longer for a place in her lover's arms?"

Rhon-Dee's already unsmiling countenance darkened under a scowl. "You," he said accusingly, "seem to be enjoying this."

Glat-Stevo spread his hands. "Why shouldn't I? I'm not in love with Her Highness Ana-Bet, ruler of all Andara."

"Are you suggesting that *I* am?"

"Suggesting it?" Glat-Stevo gave a snort of amusement. "There's none in all Andara who doesn't *know* it! You wear your heart on your forehead, Dee—and in this case hopelessly so. The handsome Had-Sudol holds Ana-Bet's heart—and dead or alive he'll never let it go."

ANGER AND pain at his friend's words were evident in Rhon-Dee's eyes. He was on the point of making some heated retort, when the cabin door was thrust unceremoniously open and the Princess Ana-Bet, breathtaking in a revealing tunic of royal green, stood there, her deep brown eyes flashing with mingled anger and impatience.

Both men sprang to their feet and came stiffly to attention, the stylus dropping from Rhon-Dee's fingers to the desktop and making a brief whisper of sound in the sudden silence as it rolled a few inches across the metal surface.

When she spoke, Ana-Bet's voice was as cold as Rhon-Dee's eyes. "Why are you sitting here?" she demanded of the commander. Before he could reply, she swept into the room and up to the desk, ignoring completely the stiff-faced Glat-Stevo. "Must I remind you," she continued imperiously, "that we are here for a reason—that every minute counts? Do you intend sending out warriors in search of Had-Sudol—or do you expect to lounge about with your feet up and your jaws flapping like those of palace slaves?"

Color burned in Rhon-Dee's lean cheeks; but his voice was quiet and contained. "Is it Her Highness' desire to take over command of this expedition?"

Ana-Bet's firm breasts pushed hard against her low-cut bodice under a sharply drawn breath. "You—you speak this way to me? I should order you whipped before the eyes of every person on these ships!"

Rhon-Dee bowed gravely. "I await Her Highness' pleasure."

The girl—she was no mere than a year or two past twenty—bit her lip in indecision and her eyes wavered and fell before the man's steady gaze. When she spoke again, her anger was gone, replaced by an almost childish petulance.

"Why do you treat me this way, Dee? You know I need you if I'm to find Had-Sudol. Why must you be difficult?"

At her words there came into Rhon-Dee's face an expression of such fawning adoration that Glat-Stevo, seeing it, felt his teeth grind in impotent rage. Damn a woman, he thought, who could thus melt down the metal of Andara's finest warrior! True, she was the planet's most beautiful woman; but beauty was evil when it could turn a man's blood to water.

Rhon-Dee said, "Twenty armed men are preparing to scout the fleet's immediate vicinity, Princess. We already have learned the air is breathable; and its pressure, while somewhat greater than that of Tarvius, will give us no discomfort. When we're certain no danger exists, the hatches will be opened and the search for Had-Sudol can begin."

The girl's brown eyes widened. "Danger? From what?"

"That we do not know—yet. But it is almost certain some form of intelligent life exists here. Just how intelligent—and how dangerous—is what we must know before we go any further with our plans."

The soft full lips of the princess curled slightly. "Always the cautious one, aren't you, Dee? In almost two days of circling this world we've seen nothing but great empty seas and vast stretches of land filled with mountains and plains and forests. Not a single city—not even a crude hut suitable for the lowest slave. Give me two warriors armed only with *kodets* and I will take the entire planet!"

"Let's hope it will he that easily done," Rhon-Dee said lightly. "Not that we'll have to conquer it all, however. According to charts found among Had-Sudol's papers, he intended to bring down his ship somewhere in this vicinity. Since this valley seems the only likely landing spot within miles, the chances are good that we should pick up some trace of him within a few days at the most."

The girl was staring closely at him as he spoke. "You don't want him found, do you, Dee?" she said with sudden directness. "Or better still, you'd like his bones found bleaching in the sun, so that I may *know* he is dead!"

Through stiffened lips Rhon-Dee muttered, "What words of mine have given Her Highness the right to so accuse me?"

"Words?" Ana-Bet snapped. "Do I need words from you? Your face, your eyes, your voice, even the set of your shoulders, tell me better than any words what you are thinking. Hear this, Rhon-Dee: I love only one man—and if it be true that he no longer lives, as you hope, then I would mate with the lowest slave before enduring the touch of your hand!"

With this, the Princess Ana-Bet whirled and stormed out of the room.

When the echoes of the slammed door were gone, Glat-Stevo's eyes dropped to his hands and he did not speak. He could picture the anguish the girl's hot words must have brought to his dearest friend, and he would not shame him by seeing it mirrored on his face...

In the silence there was a minute click as a tiny switch was thrown; then came Rhon-Dee's voice, calm and unhurried:

"Attention, all captains. Attention, all captains. Disembark your men and stand by for further orders."

CHAPTER TWO

VALAR, youthful warrior of the tribe of Polex, awoke with a start. Dimly to his ears came a distant throbbing drone, which even as his brain registered the sound, faded and was gone.

A puzzled frown creased the clear deeply tanned skin of his forehead as he drew himself erect on the high-flung branch of a jungle patriarch where he had been sleeping through the humid heat of mid-afternoon. He spent a moment or two peering through the tangle of vines, creepers and leaves partially hiding the game trail below. But nothing moved along the dusty ribbon there, and only the sound of myriad insects and the chattering of a band of long-tailed monkeys broke the silence.

Valar ran a hand thoughtfully through his shock of tousled black hair. To remain alive long in this savage world required full knowledge of everything in it; and he was well aware that nothing in his experience could explain the peculiar muted roar he had just heard. As he sought to recall the direction from which the sound had come, the belief grew that it had originated from above and toward the place where each morning Oru, the sun, rose from its sleep.

Although the air was hot, Valar felt a little shiver of cold sweep through him. Around the cave fires during the rainy season he had heard many stories of giant gods who roamed the skies and hurled great bolts of fire upon the cringing world below. Perhaps it was the voice of one of those gods which had roused him! Valar's powerful hand dropped to the stone knife thrust within the folds of his loin cloth. It might be wiser if he gave up his plan of hunting Tao, the deer, in the cool of evening and returned to the caves of his tribe.

But even as the thought came, Valar discarded it. A warrior, who ran from a mere sound, no matter how strange, was fit only for painting pictures on cave walls! Besides, as a member of the tribe, it was his duty to investigate anything that might prove to be a source of danger to his people.

Having thus rationalized his natural curiosity into something much more high-minded, Valar adjusted the coils of his grass rope across one shoulder and under the opposite arm, swung his quiver of flint-tipped arrows into place, picked up the short black-wood bow and set off resolutely through the upper terraces of the forest, moving due east.

With all the effortless grace of little Tola, the monkey, the young caveman raced along the swaying boughs from one tree to the next—now threading his way along a slender branch before leaping lithely across twenty feet of open space to grasp unerringly a trailing vine with which to swing him into the embrace of still another forest giant. Time and again his only support was his mighty hands and arms whose biceps were like banded layers of steel. Yet in all this there was no suggestion of effort—no apparent strain or tension. The dense jungle foliage seemed magically to open and close ahead and behind his flying figure, so that seldom did he brush against the riot of vegetation.

With all this speed, however, Valar was moving with the stealth of Tarka, the panther, stalking its prey. At any moment he might come upon the source of the mysterious sound which had awakened him—and it was a jungle axiom that anything strange was sure to be dangerous as well.

WHEN nearly two hours had passed without disclosing anything more deadly than the usual forest denizens, Valar began to wonder if what he had heard was no more than a figment of his imagination. Darkness was not far away, and so rapid had been his progress through the trees that he was a long way from the caves of his people. The jungle at night held no terrors for him, for he was as much at home within its inky depths as he would be surrounded by his own people. It was simply that a useless journey through a relatively unknown territory held no attraction for him.

Unconsciously he slowed his pace; and when another half-hour went by without incident he was on the point of turning back when he caught a glimpse of a break among the trees. Slowly he swung ahead, and a few moments later was poised high in a tree overlooking a narrow strip of grassland bordering the edge of a wide valley. A long-gone glacier had left a sprinkling of loose shale, rocks and boulders at the lip of the cliffs, and a family of monkeys was perched there, chattering among themselves with great excitement while peering down at the valley floor.

What the creatures saw was effectively hidden from Valar. He slid lightly to the ground, probed the grassy belt between him and the cliff top with eyes, ears and nose as highly developed as those of any jungle dweller. Very faintly he caught what might have been the murmur of many voices and irregular clanking sounds that were like nothing he had ever heard before.

The inherent caution that is so much a part of all creatures of the wild held Valar hidden within the jungle's edge for a while longer as he sought to solve by ear alone the meaning of those strange noises. But the insistent tug of curiosity finally overcame all reluctance, and knife in hand he wriggled his way through the tall grass toward the cliff's edge.

So soundless was the caveman's progress that he nearly reached his goal before the band of monkeys caught sight of him. Voicing shrill cries of anger and alarm they scampered past him in a wide circle and disappeared into the jungle. Valar froze face down where he lay, fearing that unfriendly eyes had witnessed Tola's precipitate flight and would come to investigate. But the odd sounds, louder now, went on as before; and presently he began to inch his way ahead once more.

By the time he reached the line of boulders the fading light of day ended with the abruptness common to the tropics. Valar was congratulating himself that he was now safe from prying eyes, when a vast pool of artificial light suddenly flooded the valley floor and the probing fingers of huge beacons lit up the entire sky above it.

Only an iron will and a mind that knew not the meaning of fear kept Valar from bounding to his feet and fleeing for the safety of the trees. But once the initial shock had passed and no fresh danger revealed itself, the cave youth slipped between two mammoth boulders and carefully poked his head over the edge of the sheer cliff.

The sight that met his eyes was one the young warrior was never to forget. In the glare of radiance from several portable banks of lights was a line of enormous cylinders, drawn to tapering points in front and ending bluntly in a maze of power tubes and tail fins. They lay with their bellies in the grass, nose to tail, each several hundred feet long and fully fifty feet in height. Around them, bathed in brilliant man-made light, eddied and flowed a river of strange beings clad in unknown skins of many colors that reached from neck to knee. While they were formed exactly as the people of his own tribe, Valar discovered, they were more on the frail side, their skin was far lighter in color and, with few exceptions, their hair was much shorter. The faces were as free of hair as Valar's own, but the distance was too great for him to make out the features.

THE young cave lord was enthralled. Surely here were the gods of legend and story. How he longed to descend boldly and greet them, to hear from their lips such wisdom as to make him the envy of his tribe. With the wish, however, came the pangs of doubt. Not all gods, according to tribal elders, were good. In fact, from the stories he had heard, most of them were a senselessly cruel and vicious lot who brought droughts and floods and sickness and death, and who often assumed the likeness of the great cats or deadly snakes to kill you unless you carried within your loin cloth a protective amulet. Valar himself carried a small stone marked with yellow ochre for that purpose, which he had purchased from his tribe's most venerated patriarch at the cost of two plump deer.

Valar scratched his head in puzzlement. How does one tell a friendly god from an evil one? It was a ticklish point—one that would plague mankind for thousands of years to come. Perhaps if he returned to the caves of Polex and enlisted the aid of older heads— He put the thought from him. This was his discovery. To share it with others would be to run the risk of having all glory and honor taken over by somebody else.

The hours wore on, and still Valar crouched there drinking in the scene below him. He watched the strangers as they strolled aimlessly about the towering cylinders or entered and left the lighted interiors. Some of them manned the banks of lights, while others operated the powerful beacons, shifting the blinding beams in apparently aimless patterns along the valley walls and the sky overhead. Several times Valar jerked his head back barely in time to prevent the moving rays from picking him out to the eyes below.

Later, he witnessed the return of several hunting parties bearing a number of carcasses of Tao, the deer. Fires were kindled near each cylinder and soon the mouth-watering scent of grilled meat rose to Valar's nostrils reminding him that he had not eaten since mid-morning. But even the claws of a healthy appetite could not drag the cave youth from his vantage point. From the forest depths behind him rose the nightly chorus: the coughing grunt of Kraga, the lion, and Conta, his mate; the shrill scream of Shanda, the leopard, as he made his kill; the purring growl of Tarka, the panther, as he fed upon the body of some succulent grass-eater. So accustomed to these sounds was Valar that he heard them only subconsciously, but there was none of them that instinct and experience did not weigh as a possible threat.

Once a stirring in the grasses, so faint that an ordinary ear could never have caught it, brought him around and ready, knife clenched in a muscular fist. But the sound was not repeated and he turned back to his rapt study of the valley below.

At last the activity there lessened as the strange beings began to straggle into the monstrous cylinders. Cooking fires were smothered and one by one the searchlights winked out and the banks of portable floodlights dimmed and went black. Sentries, two to each space liner, took up positions near the main hatchways; and Valar noticed that each man held a short glistening tube curved at one end to fit the hand. Some kind of weapon, he decided, and wondered at the form of death it would deal out.

All during his lonely vigil a plan had been forming in the caveman's mind. At first he was hardly aware of it, but as the strangers sought their beds and the lights went out, leaving the camp in partial darkness, it began to take on concrete lines. It was a plan that was worse than foolhardy—and therein lay its chief charm!

Why not slip into the very midst of the encampment and observe its wonders at close hand?

The longer he thought about it, the less reckless such an attempt seemed. By carefully circling the area he could come up to those huge man-made cliffs from the side opposite to where the sentries were posted. He would be reasonably safe from discovery, for Mua, the moon, had not yet risen to roam the night sky; that plus his own ability to move as soundlessly as a shadow should be protection aplenty.

Backing away from the rocky rim, Valar rose to his feet and flitted lightly southward until he was well below the point where the last of the cylinders lay. Satisfied that no eye, however keen, could observe him, he slid lithely over the brink of the valley and swarmed down the sheer rock with an ease and surefootedness that would have been incredible even in the full light of day.

Once he reached the level floor of the valley, Valar's approach to the rear ship was as silent as it was swift. Within a few minutes after reaching solid ground he arrived at the unguarded side of the towering craft and was running an inquisitive hand along its silvery underside.

It was Valar's first contact with metal of any kind, and its chill smooth feel brought an involuntary murmur of awe to his lips. Slowly he moved along the giant craft's entire length, lost in wonder at the miracle of its construction.

So engrossed was the cave youth that his first inkling of danger came when a strong light struck him full in the eyes, momentarily blinding him. With the quickness of thought he turned to flee—only to pitch headlong as muscular arms caught him around the legs!

CHAPTER THREE

HE AWAKENED late that morning. Already Oru was above the line of trees to the east, and from the clearing below the caves came the sounds of women at their never ending tasks and the shrill voices of children at play.

He dozed for a while longer, half-awake, until the pangs of hunger began to grow uncomfortably. Rising from his pallet of skins, he crossed the large and comparatively light and airy cave and stepped out onto a ledge of rock nearly a hundred feet above the clearing.

"Ho there!" he shouted.

Instantly all activity ceased on the ground below. The women looked up almost fearfully and the children fell silent. Even a group of warriors ceased their endless bragging.

"Where is my food?" cried the man on the ledge. "I am hungry!"

A woman who had been removing the hair from a deer skin dropped the stone scraper guiltily and ran into one of the caves. Only then did life below take up its normal course, but more subdued now as though still under the spell of the man standing high up the cliff side.

Satisfied that he would soon be fed, the man turned and entered his subterranean quarters. Near the rear wall a small spring bubbled along the stone floor before disappearing underground again. Removing the circle of panther skin from about his hips, the man bathed himself in the cold water, shivering at its bite.

As he crouched there by the small stream and dried himself with handfuls of dead grasses, he caught a glimpse of his face reflected by the water. His long imprisonment had changed him but little, he decided. His gray eyes were still clear and steady; his face, a bit fuller through lack of activity, was undeniably handsome. Systematic exercises had kept his tall slender body supple and strong, and long hours of sunning himself on the outer ledge had tanned his skin almost to blackness.

If only he had something to do—someone to talk with. He marveled again that sheer boredom had not driven him mad long before this. There was no hope of his ever returning to his own world, for the space ship that had brought him here lay wrecked beyond repair where it had crashed on that long-gone day when he had landed on this miserable planet!

The wild men who had found him crumpled beside his ship would have slain him where he lay had not older heads among them urged caution. It was clear, they pointed out, that he was a god. To kill him might well bring destruction to the entire tribe. But the younger and more hot-headed members argued that a god would never have permitted himself to fall into their hands in the first place—a point countered by the statement that this might be some sort of test by the gods to learn if the tribe of Ulgo was worthy of life.

Ulgo, himself, had solved the dilemma. They would put him in one of the high caves where escape was impossible for a mortal. If he vanished, then he was indeed a god; if he grew old and died, then he was human and who would care?

For the first year of his captivity Had-Sudol, nobleman of Andara, was treated with the utmost respect. The aged crone who twice daily brought him food was so overcome with awe that she was barely able to perform her task. Had there been a way for him to descend to the ground or scale the remaining distance to the top of the cliffs he would long since have escaped. But the lack of foot—or hand—holds on the sheer rock sealed him up as effectively as the thickest stone walls could have done.

FROM THE first, Had-Sudol had spoken kindly to the old woman who brought his food, although he realized she could not understand his words. When he did so, she would shrink back fearfully, put down the bowls of food and dash for the outer ledge to be drawn up by a rope to the cliff's rim.

However, when the first year had passed and he had not transformed her into the likeness of Cretah, the hyena, or blasted her with sky fire, she began to relax sufficiently to answer his greeting. From this beginning they slowly progressed to where she was teaching him the language of the cavemen.

Only a moon or so ago she had brought him a bit of disquieting news. Her wrinkled face seemed even more troubled than usual as she had placed a portion of well-cooked deer flesh in his hands, and when, at his urging, she told him what was troubling her, her voice quavered with something more than age.

"There are those among the warriors who say you are no god," she had said. "They argue that were you such, you would long ago have gone back to the skies from whence you came. They say you should be put to death—that they are weary of hunting food to keep you fat while their own families often go hungry."

His smile had been grave. "You know I'm not a god, Koka. Many times I have told you so. Why do you not tell them?"

Her eyes, he realized, had glistened with what could have been mistaken for tears if he had not known her better. "I will tell them nothing! They do not want me because I am old and useless. There is little time left for me, and without you to care for I would have nothing to do but sit alone and wait to die." She had paused briefly, staring at him out of beady black eyes, then smiled, revealing toothless black gums. "Because you say you are no god does not keep you from being one. True, you have remained here three summers. But what is time to a god? Perhaps it is thus that you test the tribe of Ulgo!"

SO DEEP in thought was Had-Sudol that he failed completely to hear the slither of rope against the rock outside his cave. But the sound of a stealthy footstep behind him broke through his preoccupation and he straightened and whirled in one smooth swift motion.

Standing there was a girl—a girl lovely beyond belief!

The young nobleman's arms fell limply to his sides and his jaw sagged with open astonishment. And then he saw that the girl was staring with frank admiration at his naked body, and he caught up the skin of Tarka and fastened it about his middle, his fingers unsteady. The girl's face flamed then until it was no less red than his own.

"Who are you?" he demanded sharply.

She held out a stone bowl in which were bits of stewed flesh and fruit fresh from the trees. "I have brought you food," she said, her low, faintly husky voice unsteady.

Automatically Had-Sudol took the bowl from her, his eyes never leaving her face. Her hair, falling in rich profusion to her flawless shoulders, was the warm gold of sunlight—a hue almost unheard of among the dark-skinned cave dwellers. Her eyes were direct, intelligent and so deeply blue as to seem almost black. High cheekbones with faint hollows beneath, a small shapely nose above bewitching lips, a firm rounded chin that hinted of a rebellious nature, skin more golden than tanned—these made up the perfection and vitality of her face. She was somewhat taller than average, long and slender in the legs, with the pelt of Shanda, the leopard, both concealing and emphasizing the softly rounded glory of hips and breasts.

Had-Sudol wet suddenly dry lips and his smile was an almost obvious effort. "Who are you?" he repeated.

There must have been something in his expression that he was unaware of; for suddenly the girl retreated a pace or two and glanced uneasily over her shoulder toward the cave entrance.

"Wait," the young man said quickly. "Don't go. You are—"

The rush of words stopped abruptly as Had-Sudol realized he had been about to say to this savage half-naked cave girl words he had never spoken to any woman.

They stood there unmoving, looking deep into each other's eyes, in a silence as electric as a tropical rainstorm. And then the man from Andara deliberately broke the spell.

Reaching into the stone bowl, he scooped up several bits of meat and began to eat. "Where," he said, "is Koka? Always before she was the one to bring me my food."

"She is dead," the girl said indifferently. "When my mother tried to wake her this morning, she was cold and stiff. And so they took her out and heaped stones over her."

Had-Sudol winced, not only because his only friend in the tribe was dead, but at the lack of feeling in the voice of this lovely creature. He said wonderingly: "Was Koka of your family?"

"She was the mother of my mother."

"Doesn't it matter to you that she is dead?"

The girl obviously did not understand what prompted the question. "She saw many summers. Does one live forever?"

Had-Sudol shrugged and gave it up. What could you expect from savages? He bit one of the round balls of fruit. "You haven't told me your name," he pointed out.

"I am Duleen, daughter of Ulgo who is chief of the tribe."

"Duleen..." He repeated the name lingeringly. "It is a lovely name—almost as lovely as you."

She reddened with a mixture of pleasure and confusion and made no reply.

"Why," Had-Sudol asked, "does the daughter of a chief bring food to a prisoner?"

"Who else would be permitted to serve a god?"

He gulped down the rest of the food and put down the bowl instead of handing it to the girl. With a bit of dried grass he wiped his hands and lips, smiling faintly at Duleen's uncertain expression.

"Do you think I'm a god?" he asked.

"Yes," she said simply. "Only a god could come out of the sky."

His heart was beginning to pound uncontrollably. Almost of its own accord his hand reached out and caught her by the wrist. "You are beautiful, Duleen," he whispered hoarsely.

She stood stiff and unmoving, her warm lips slightly parted, her breasts rising and falling under ragged breathing.

And then Had-Sudol swept the lovely girl savagely into his arms and pressed his lips firmly against hers.

For a brief intoxicating moment she yielded to his passionate caress. But for only a moment. With a half stifled gasp, she wrenched free of his embrace and lashed out with one clawing hand. Nails bit into his cheek bringing blood and he fell back, voicing a startled cry of pain. Before he could recover, the girl whirled out of his reach and was running for the outer ledge, her golden hair flying.

"Duleen!" he shouted. "Wait I didn't mean—"

He was alone in the cave. By the time he reached the ledge the girl was swarming hand-over-hand up a single strand of grass rope anchored at the cliff top. His first impulse was to follow to make her understand that he had acted so only out of a loneliness three years had made unbearable. But immediately he realized such a move would be useless, if not actually dangerous. The guards constantly on duty above the caves would be armed where he was not; they could kill or recapture him, depending on how they felt about the matter. Or, he thought ruefully, the girl might do the job for them. In her anger she might loosen the rope while he still climbed—and plunge him a hundred feet to the ground below.

Duleen, daughter of Ulgo, disappeared with a breathtaking display of bare legs and shapely thighs, and a moment later the dangling rope too was gone. His mind a welter of conflicting emotions. Had-Sudol turned and walked slowly back into his cell.

CHAPTER FOUR

AS HE FELL to the ground under the impact of an unseen attacker, Valar twisted savagely aside, freeing his legs from the vise-like grip. Cat-like he came to his feet, only to feel hands close about one ankle and seek to bring him down again. Forgetting the knife at his belt, the cave youth brought a clenched fist down in a chopping motion that, had it landed squarely, would have snapped the other's spine like a dry twig. Instead, the blow landed glancingly on a shoulder, bringing a shrill cry of anguish; and before Valar could strike again, two more of Rhon-Dee's warriors were upon him.

The battle, which followed, was short and savage. Brought to his knees under the fresh attack, the man from the caves came erect with the full weight of two heavily built men across his back. Reaching over his shoulder, he fastened one hand in the folds of a tunic, tore one of the figures away and flung it aside with a single sweep of his arm. There was a dull crunching sound as bone met metal—and the odds had shrunk to two to one.

A single shake of his mighty shoulders freed Valar from the weight of the second enemy. Snatching the stone knife from his loin cloth, he brought the razor-keen blade around in a sweeping arc that caught the third warrior full in the throat and nearly decapitated him. Blood spurted, staining the caveman red from chest to knees as he avoided the crumpling figure and turned to run.

He was too late! A living wall of fighting men, aroused by the sounds of conflict, rose in Valar's path and flung themselves upon him. Several felt the agony of knife wounds before the weapon was torn from his grasp, then the butt of a heat pistol crashed sickeningly against his skull—and the young caveman knew no more.

* * *

FOR THE rest of the morning Duleen went about her usual duties in a daze. It seemed that she could still feel the strong arms of the god around her, the flaming touch of his lips on her own, the heat of his body burning into her flesh like the rays of Oru.

It was not that she failed to understand what was happening to her. Eighteen summers among the caves and jungles of her untamed world had given Duleen more than an inkling of the intimate relationship between male and female. Most of the young men—and many an older one!—of her father's tribe had shown clearly that they desired her. But where, before, it had left her unmoved, the brief encounter with the handsome young captive had changed all that. Just thinking of him tore her between ecstasy and confusion. She never wanted to see him again—and the hours were dragging until she might again bring him his food.

No! She would not go near him. Let somebody else wait on him! How could she go back there after what he had done? He could starve as far as she was concerned!

Moments later she was staring up at the sky, wondering at the slowness of Oru's passage.

By mid-afternoon Duleen was as tense and jumpy as one of the great cats prowling the jungle. She had gone to the spring for water for the cooking pots, when Bulat, a hunter of the tribe, came bursting into the clearing breathless with excitement.

"The gods have come!" he shouted. "I saw them! The gods are here!"

Instantly he was surrounded by an excited throng of warriors and women. The word "gods" had electrified them all. Hearing it, Duleen, her mind on the captive god, dropped the huge gourd filled with water and ran to join the others. Her father was already there, tall, hawk-nosed, commanding.

"Has Oru cooked your head, Bulat?" the chief snapped. "What is this talk of gods?"

"I tell you I saw them!" the hunter cried. "They came down like Keta, the eagle, in great hollow rocks as long as the highest tree. From the sky they came, lightly as a drifting leaf, until they reached the ground. At first these great shining rocks lay there resting, then holes appeared in their sides and many gods came out and walked among the grasses of the valley. For a time I watched them; then I hurried here to tell you."

THERE WAS a murmur of superstitious awe from some of his listeners and expressions of fear were plain on several faces among the women. But Ulgo indicated he was strongly skeptical.

"Where are those shining rocks?" he asked.

"A short march toward where Oru sleeps."

"And you say there were many of these gods?"

"Many times the number of a man's fingers and toes," Bulat declared. "And those, I think, were not all. Others must have remained within the long rocks."

"How large were these gods?" Some of the chief's doubt was fading under the promptness and certainty of the hunter's words.

"Much like the god we keep here," Bulat said. "And they wore strange skins like the one he wore when we found him."

At this, the nervousness of Bulat's audience increased markedly, and one of the tribe's old—and presumably wise—men raised his voice. "They have come to free their brother," he said quaveringly. "They will come here and kill us all unless we run into the jungle and hide until they are gone."

An undercurrent of agreement to the proposal swept the crowd, forcing the wily chief to act promptly or be caught up in a stampede he would be helpless to contain.

"Are we like Cretah, the hyena, to slink into the bushes, afraid of what we have not even seen? Let us go and look at these gods before we talk of running away."

His words brought a sudden melting back of the men nearest him. Ulgo's face purpled with rage; but before he could find his voice again, the old man spoke up a second time.

"We must free the captive god," he said solemnly, "that he may return to his brothers and tell them we did not harm him. Then will they return to the sky and leave us in peace."

As befitted a chief, Ulgo would have none of this craven suggestion. "No!" he shouted. "He would only lead them to our caves that they might slaughter us. Instead we will kill him and throw his body into their faces. Thus will they know that the warriors of Ulgo fear neither god nor man!"

Duleen, listening at the outer fringes of the group, felt cold fear close about her heart at her father's words. Tears stung her eyes and a protest rose to her lips. But she bit back the words because she knew nothing she could say would change things and because she was not actually sure that she wanted Had-Sudol to live. Or, she thought wildly, maybe she was sure and refused to admit it!

After a heated argument it was decided that Ulgo and ten of his warriors would go to the valley and get some idea of just how many gods were there. The general feeling seemed to be that Had-Sudol would have to die as an object lesson to his kind, but that his death would be delayed until the chief and his ten warriors returned.

IT WAS a worried and confused girl, therefore, who slid down the rope to Had-Sudol's cell later that afternoon. As she reached the ledge, a crude stone bowl of food held under one arm, the splendid figure of the young Andaraian appeared in the cave opening.

"Duleen!" he exclaimed. "You came back after all!"

The relief and happiness in his voice went through her with a pleasant little shock. Silently she extended the stone bowl, but her trembling fingers gave her away. He brushed it aside and she was in his arms.

At last he put her gently from him and looked deep into her eyes while her breathing grew calm again and her lips ceased their quivering.

"I love you, Duleen." The words were barely a whisper, but there was no doubting their sincerity, even as his mind shouted that a nobleman of Andara could not say such things to a wild girl of the caves.

In answer, the girl dropped her face into her hands and began to cry long wracking sobs that shook her slender shoulders like a reed in a high wind.

"What is it, my darling?" He took hold of her tenderly and drew her into the shelter of the cave. "Does my love hurt you so much?"

She shook her head wildly, still sobbing. "Th-they are going to kill y-you!"

She felt his body stiffen and heard the sharp intake of his breath. A hand caught her under the chin and lifted her face until he could see into her eyes again. "Kill me?" he repeated, his voice calm. "Who is going to kill me, Duleen?"

"My father. He says you will tell the other gods where we are and they will come here and slay us all."

"'Other gods?'" the man repeated, puzzled. "What other gods?"

"They appeared less than half a sun ago," she told him. "From out of the sky, in long shining rocks. Bulat saw them as they came to rest in the valley and from them came gods such as you."

For a moment it was as though her words had turned him to stone. Then he shouted aloud with a mixture of relief and exultation. "They came! By Novah, *they came!* Ana-Bet must have—"

The rush of words stopped abruptly as the picture of Andara's princess as last he had seen her rose unbidden to his mind's eye.

IT WAS during the days, three years before, when he had been the fair-haired boy of the court of Tar-Jando, Ana-Bet's father and emperor of Andara, the most powerful nation on all Tarvius. Had-Sudol was in his early twenties then—a handsome, devil-may-care youngster who knew more about flying-ships than any expert had a right to. He built them from the ground up, he tinkered with their motors, adding refinements and inventions of his own until, almost singlehandedly he had torn apart the air force of one of Andara's neighbors during one of the intermittent wars between them.

And it was about that time when Tar-Jando's only child, the princess Ana-Bet, had indicated very clearly that she had marked Had-Sudol for her own. She was no more than eighteen years of age—a leggy, big-eyed imperious combination of a girl and woman whose moods were as stormy and unpredictable as they were brief. She made a continuous habit of showing up wherever the young airman was—watching him for hour after hour while he developed the principle of harnessing magnetic fields as a source of power. His attitude was pretty much that of a brother toward a younger sister; and while this was a relationship far from what Ana-Bet had in mind, she was content to bide her time, confident that eventually he would take his nose out of the mazes of machinery long enough to realize she was a very beautiful and desirable woman.

And then one day Had-Sudol took her into his confidence. He had, it seemed, solved the last barrier between interplanetary travel, and he proposed to set out for Tarvius' nearest neighbor—the green world called Eonia. No one else, he told her, was to know his plans until after he had taken off.

Ana-Bet was intelligent enough to know that opposing him in his mad venture would only cost her what slight inroads she had already made on his heart. So she beat back her fear, helped him obtain supplies in secret, and at his request hid away a duplicate set of plans for Andara's military in case he did not return.

Not until the cold gray dawn when they stood alone beside his small one-man flyer, its nose pointed skyward, did Ana-Bet betray her love for Had-Sudol. As he said his goodbyes and turned to enter the waiting craft, she had thrown her arms tightly about his neck and kissed him over and over again, whispering in a very broken manner that she loved him and would not ever know happiness until he returned safely to her. Touched by the unashamed ardor of her love, swayed by the dramatic setting of the moment, the young man had responded with equal ardor, murmuring words that gave Ana-Bet permanent claim to his heart.

Now, standing on a high stone ledge overlooking a savage world, another girl warm in his arms, Had-Sudol, nobleman of Andara, realized for the first time that gratitude and a momentary affection, not actual love, had been responsible for his promise to Ana-Bet.

The knowledge gave him no comfort. If, as seemed likely, she had brought an expedition so vast a distance to find him, it was because she still loved him.

What was he to do? He could not remain here; the cavemen would kill him. Yet to return to Andara with Ana-Bet would mean spending the rest of his life with a woman he did not love. He knew the princess too well to suppose she would willingly transport a rival to Andara, and he was equally sure she would insist on holding him to his promise to her. Refusal might well mean his death, knowing the princess as he did...

Duleen, puzzled and a little uneasy by his strained silence, stirred slightly in his arms and he tightened them almost convulsively about her bare shoulders. By Novah, he would not give the cave girl up!

"Listen to me, my darling," he whispered. "Do you love me as I love you?"

In answer she drew his head down and pressed her lips tightly against his own. After a long ecstatic moment he lifted his head and smiled down into her eyes.

"Then this," he said, "is what you must do…"

CHAPTER FIVE

THE CLAMOR of an alarm bell brought Rhon-Dee bolt upright in his bunk. With the smooth ease of a man used to alarms in the night he swung his legs to the floor and into sandals even as his fingers found his tunic. In the corridor outside was the pounding of feet as the ship's crew raced to battle stations.

As he flung open his cabin door and started out, Rhon-Dee spotted the tall broad-shouldered figure of Glat-Stevo coming toward him.

"What's going on, Stevo?" the commander demanded.

"Seems the guards have caught some sort of spy. Found him lurking about outside this ship."

"A human?"

The captain shrugged. "I haven't seen him yet—if 'him' is the right word. I called for a general alarm on all ships. Just in case there's more of them skulking around."

"Where is this spy?" Rhon-Dee asked.

"They took him to the ship hospital. I understand they had to knock him over the head with a kodet butt before he could be handled. Strong as ten men, I hear. Killed two of the guards before being subdued."

"Let's have a look at him."

The two officers mounted a ladder to the third level and along the corridor to a small gleaming white room. On a table was the body of an almost naked man of tremendous physical strength, to judge from the way he was built. Even unconscious, his muscles appeared to be as hard as metal. His head was large and perfectly formed, the face singularly handsome even by Tarviusian standards, the smooth clear skin darkly tanned. The eyes were closed, and thick black hair reaching almost to his shoulders fell loosely across one smoothly scraped cheek.

"Human, all right," Glat-Stevo muttered. "In fact the best looking example I can remember having seen."

A thin-faced man in the long white robe of a healer was bent over the unconscious figure applying an unguent of some kind to a nasty looking gash on one side of the leonine head. Across from him two guards, kodets ready in their right hands, watched without expression.

"Is he going to come out of it?" Rhon-Dee asked.

The healer nodded. "He took a nasty crack but he's got a head as hard as the side of this ship. Better bind him down or he's liable to come out of it fighting."

Glat-Stevo gestured to one of the guards. The man holstered his weapon, came up to the table and drew two broad bands of leather, attached to the sides of the metal slab, across the chest of the unconscious man.

A moment later the captive stirred and opened his eyes. At sight of his surroundings and the man bending over him, he shot up one mighty hand and closed it about the healer's throat. The white-robed Andaran sought wildly to free that terrible grip but he might as well have tried to beat in the side of a mountain. Not until one of the guards stepped forward and brought his kodet butt down on the steel wrist did those incredible fingers relax their hold. The healer collapsed half conscious, livid marks on the skin of his throat. As he fell, the captive lunged up in one superhuman burst of strength that brought a complaining creak from the metal table and tested the straps across his body to their limit. But they held—and the wild man fell back.

"Ask him who he is, Stevo," Rhon-Dee said.

The officer stared at him blankly. "You don't think he'd understand our language, do you?"

"Probably not. But let's make sure."

THERE WAS sudden and sharp silence in the room as Glat-Stevo approached the table. The eyes watching him from that point were a light gray that seemed nearly as opaque as paint. Smooth pliant muscles rippled as bronzed arms tensed to defend their owner.

"Don't get excited, my friend," Glat-Stevo said, his voice calm and unhurried. He stopped just beyond the prisoner's reach. "What is your name? What do they call you?"

The gray eyes stared back at him without expression. The nostrils of the generous clean-lined nose twitched a little but that was the only reaction to the captain's words.

"No use, Rhon-Dee," Glat-Stevo said over his shoulder. "For all his human look and physical development he's no more than a wild animal. Evidently this world is still too young for man to have reached our own stage. Maybe our first ancestors on Tarvius were much the same as this specimen."

The white-robed healer, still on the floor beside the table, lurched to his hands and knees. Moaning softly, he began to crawl across the room, then stood erect long enough to collapse again, this time into a metal chair. Nobody paid any attention to him.

Commander Rhon-Dee rubbed the side of his jaw thoughtfully. "We've got to find out if he was alone or a scout for a raiding party," he said finally. "Have one of the technicians bring in a translavox."

"Doubt if it'll do much good," Glat-Stevo said. "They only work on a higher intelligence, you know."

"We don't know how intelligent he is. This will be a way to find out."

The captain gave a brief order to one of the guards, who saluted briskly and went out. A moment later he was back, followed by a short fat man of middle age pushing a complex square of wires, tubes, coils and switches mounted on a wheeled table. At sight of the forbidding looking wild man strapped to the slab, the technician halted abruptly.

"Well?" Rhon-Dee said impatiently. "What are you waiting for? There's your subject; get him ready for questioning."

The technician pushed the machine forward another inch, then stopped a second time, eyeing the unrestrained arms dubiously. "He appears capable of resistance, Commander," he said in a voice that could have been steadier.

Rhon-Dee made a sign to the guard. The man drew his kodet, set a tiny rheostat in the base of its grip and leveled the muzzle at the captive. There followed a brief crackling sound; the caveman's body jerked spasmodically once and then slumped back in the limpness of unconsciousness.

Quickly the guard put away his weapon and stepped to the table and readjusted the straps so that they confined the arms as well as the giant frame. Reassured, the technician now wheeled his compact mechanism up to the table and attached a set of electrodes to the captive's temples. From the electrodes ran two fine wires ending in two incredibly sensitive button microphones. From the first pair of wires depended two others that disappeared into the body of the translavox.

At instructions from Rhon-Dee, Glat-Stevo took over. He drew a chair up beside the table where the captive still lay unconscious. The captain fastened one of the button microphones to his own ear and held the other in his hand, waiting.

The caveman's eyes fluttered open and burned into Glat-Stevo's with such unmasked hatred that the captain felt a prickle of fear for the first time since he could remember.

ORIGINALLY the translavox had been designed to read the thoughts of enemy spies who did not want their thoughts known and who were able successfully to endure torture. When, as a means of circumventing the machine, agents started getting their messages in code, refinements had been added that arranged even coded thoughts into familiar words. From this point, it was a short step to improving the machine to where it could work in reverse: enabling someone who spoke no known language to understand that of the Andarans.

Depressing a tiny button on the mechanism, Glat-Stevo said, "Who are you?" into the microphone he was holding.

Open astonishment dropped the captive's jaw. He did not move or speak, but almost at once Glat-Stevo said to Rhon-Dee: "He understands me. And he does not know how to shield his thoughts. His name is Valar."

The commander nodded. "See what else he can tell you."

Glat-Stevo was about to put another question to the man on the table when the corridor room opened and the princess Ana-Bet swept into the room. The pale green tunic she wore set off the luxuriant glory of her jet black hair and the liquid depths of brown eyes. She paused just inside the door, frowning slightly at sight of the tremendous young man on the table.

"They told me you were in here," she said to Rhon-Dee. "What does this mean?"

In a few words the commander explained what had happened. "We want to find out," he finished, "if there is danger of attack from others of his kind. Also, if he knows anything of Had-Sudol."

From where he lay on the table, Valar watched the scene around him with awed wonder. He knew that he was helpless in the hands of gods; but the knowledge brought no feeling of panic, for he realized that, physically at least, he was more than a match for several of them at one time. Nor were they immortal; he was sure that the warrior whose neck his knife had torn was dead. No, it was only in the strange things they possessed that their advantage lay. Like the things fastened to his head and to the thin vines leading to the ear and mouth of the god seated next to him. He had heard the god speak strange sounding words, which his own ears did not understand but which, in his mind, were in the language of his own tribe.

From the corners of his eyes Valar stared at the girl who had just entered this white cave. He saw how humbly these gods treated her and his lip curled slightly. Did the gods allow a woman to rule them, then? True, she was beautiful beyond any woman he had ever seen before. But she was still a woman—fit only to prepare food and cure the pelts of jungle beasts for the use of warriors.

Yet there was something about her... His eyes dwelt appreciatively on her long, slender, delicately rounded limbs—on the smooth swell of her hips, the narrow waist, the mystic enchantment of firm breasts, the delicate column of her throat.

An emotion new to Valar but as old as the universe he knew nothing about was taking form within him. Suddenly he wanted to put a hand on her, to stroke her hair, to press his mouth against those full red lips...

VALAR SWALLOWED hard against a formless and unfamiliar lump in his throat and shifted his gaze to the girl's face—and found her staring directly into his eyes. Their glances met, locked, held—and it was the princess who first looked away, a dull wave of red sweeping up from her neck and into her cheeks.

"He seems to be a handsome beast," she said carelessly to Rhon-Dee. "See what you can find out from him."

Once more Glat-Stevo began to question the young cave lord. "You have told me your name is Valar. Where do you live?"

Again Valar heard words he did not understand but whose meaning was clear to his mind. He said, "The woman is good to look upon. Does she belong to you?"

Despite himself, Glat-Stevo grinned.

Ana-Bet must indeed be a revelation to this untamed giant. Well, better men had fallen under her spell. With an effort he erased the smile. "You must answer my questions," he said. "Where do you live?"

"In the caves of Polex," Valar replied indifferently.

"Where are they?"

"I will not tell you that."

"You have already told me; you cannot control your thoughts."

Valar blinked, puzzled.

"Are there many of you?" Glat-Stevo asked.

"As many as the leaves of the forest."

"Where are the warriors of your tribe?"

"They are waiting for you to leave the shelter of your rocks. Then they will fall upon you and kill you all!

After a moment's silence Glat-Stevo spoke again. "You are lying. You could not understand how I know that, but this—" he pointed to the squat machine—"tells me such things. I know that you came here alone and that none of your people know where you are."

Valar grunted. "They will find out," he said. "When I do not return they will hunt for me. Then they will kill you."

"With what?" Glat-Stevo said with quiet amusement. "The crude kind of weapons we took from you?"

"You will see!" But the doubt in Valar's tone was unmistakable.

The captain abruptly switched the subject. "Tell me, Valar, are there other tribes such as yours near here?"

The caveman moved a shoulder. "There are others. I do not know where. I heard once that farther toward the place where Oru rises another tribe has its caves. I do not know this for I have never been beyond this valley."

Glat-Stevo eyed him steadily for a long time before he asked his next question. The translavox informed him the wild man's answers were true; now that he was giving such co-operation, his next answer might cut short the expedition's stay on this insane planet.

"Have you," he said suddenly, "ever seen men like us before?"

"No," Valar said absently. It was evident he was becoming bored. His eyes were back on the Princess Ana-

Bet, causing the translavox to give Glat-Stevo a confused jumble of thoughts running through the captive's mind.

HE DISENGAGED the two tiny microphones and rose from the chair. The technician came forward, removed the electrodes and wheeled the machine from the room.

"Anything we can use, Stevo?" Rhon-Dee said.

"I doubt it. Evidently he caught sight of our ships just before they landed and came to investigate. I'm satisfied that we're the first civilized people he's ever seen—which would tend to prove he knows nothing of the noble Had-Sudol."

"Then he's no further use to us?"

"Probably not."

The commander turned away indifferently. "Then have a couple of the guards take him out somewhere and kill him." He took the arm of the princess. "Shall I see you to your quarters, Your Highness?"

At the door, Ana-Bet turned back impulsively and looked searchingly at the splendid figure on the table. He was watching her again, and even across the room she could see something in the depths of his eyes that sent tiny feet scampering up her spine.

"Why kill him, Rhon-Dee?" she said slowly. "Why shouldn't he be released unharmed?"

The commander tried valiantly to keep an impassive expression but his eyes gave him away. Clearly they indicated that she must have lost her senses. "Your Highness was not informed, of course, that this barbarian slew two of our men before he was captured. "

"What of it? Surely you would not refuse anyone the right to defend himself."

Rhon-Dee's lips stiffened into a straight line. "Also, were we to allow him to go, he would return with his men to attack us."

"Does the prospect frighten you?" she asked with poisonous sweetness.

He flushed clear to the roots of his hair. "If Her Highness will instruct me," he said harshly.

Instead, Ana-Bet glanced at the stiff-backed Glat-Stevo. "Have the wild man locked up somewhere," she said. "Perhaps I will question him myself in the morning before I decide what is to be done with him."

CHAPTER SIX

HAD-SUDOL lay belly-flat on the narrow ledge outside his lofty, lonely cell. In the clearing below burned a roaring fire of dry branches, its leaping yellow flames pushing back the impenetrable blackness of a jungle night.

For a long time now he had lain there, watching the silhouetted figures of the women and old men of Ulgo's tribe as they milled uncertainly about the blaze. A handful of warriors leaned uneasily on their spears, eyes rolling nervously at the fringes of nocturnal jungle nearby. Now and then the voice of one of the great cats tore apart the brooding silence and sent the cave people huddling closer to the fire as though its heat might ward off the chill of fear sweeping over them.

The young nobleman's fingers drummed nervously against the stone. Why didn't she come? Already she was more than an hour late. It was at least three hours ago that Ulgo and his ten warriors had returned from their scouting trip. Had-Sudol had watched a new force assemble shortly before dusk, and not long afterward the chief and more than a hundred heavily armed warriors—almost the entire fighting strength of the tribe—had disappeared into the mouth of a game trail toward the west.

It seemed incredible to Had-Sudol that they might actually be preparing to attack the visitors from Andara. As mighty as the cavemen were physically, their muscles and puny, crude weapons would be worse than useless against the terrible armaments of the Andarans.

But there were more urgent matters to worry about. Slowly the fear began to rise in him that Duleen had suffered a change of heart, that she regretted giving her love to one whom she must now look upon as an enemy of her people. A vision of her as she had looked while in his arms rose to plague him. The clinging, silken sheen of golden hair against his caressing fingers, the warmth of her softly curved body against his own, the mingled fire and benediction of her quivering mouth as she returned his kisses... Had-Sudol clenched his fists until the nails dug painfully into perspiring palms.

From behind him a slight sound brought the young man quickly to his feet. In the faint reflection of the firelight below he made out the slender, briefly-clad figure of Ulgo's daughter.

An instant later she was in his arms. "Duleen, Duleen," he whispered brokenly, all doubt forgotten. "I knew you would come!"

She placed soft fingers against his lips to halt the tumbling words. "It was not easy. I thought the guards at the top of the cliff would never go away. I finally told them they were needed below—that I would keep watch for a while. The elders fear that the gods may attack us while our warriors are away."

Had-Sudol glanced uneasily toward the fire below. "Then we must hurry if we are to get away before they come back.'

The girl stared at the dark line of towering trees beyond the clearing and shivered a little in his embrace. "The jungle is no place to be at night," she murmured. "Even our bravest fighters dare not enter it unless many of them are together."

"We will go only a little way," the man said. "Then we can climb into a tree and wait until the night has passed. Once Oru rises we will hurry on and join my friends."

Still the girl held back. "Your friends," she said. "Will they like me? I am so different from them."

"They will love you as I do!" Had-Sudol declared fervently. "You will see!"

But even as he spoke the words, a tiny nagging doubt pried at his mind. Would they accept this half-naked primitive as unconditionally as he had? The thought of her in the intrigue-ridden court of Andara, filled with its posturing opportunists, made him wince.

And Ana-Bet? How would she take this rebuff? How would she react to finding that this blonde savage had taken the man she loved? With cold and deadly fury—unless her entire nature had changed since last he saw her...

For the first time Had-Sudol began to question this suddenly born love for the cave girl. Perhaps he did not really love her. It was another emotion entirely—one brought on by the sheer loneliness of three dreary years cut off from the companionship of everybody other than an old, old woman.

The shrill scream of a panther from the forest depths beyond the fire jerked him from his reverie. "Come, Duleen," he said, almost harshly. "Let's get out of here."

A moment later the girl was disappearing into the night above him, drawing herself up lithely, hand over hand, along a slender strand of grass rope anchored somewhere overhead. He waited until the rope swung free, then slowly he began to follow, grunting a little with the effort, for it had been a long time since be had tried anything so strenuous.

But the hours of exercise during his years of imprisonment paid off. Presently he dragged himself over the lip of the escarpment and rose gingerly to his feet.

A smooth warm hand came out of the blanket of blackness around him, caught his fingers in a reassuring grip. "This way," Duleen whispered close to his ear. "Follow me."

Blindly Had-Sudol gave himself over to her guidance. They took a few steps, when suddenly a hoarse voice shouted almost in their faces and simultaneously the haft of a spear caught the Andaran a ringing blow alongside the head, bringing him to his knees. A fog rolled into his brain as he fell and cutting through it came Duleen's cry of fear.

*   *   *

"BUT WHY, Ana-Bet?" Rhon-Dee's brow was creased into deep lines of complete bafflement. "He's no more than an animal. Why waste a full day of a technician's time on this—this freak?"

The commander of the expedition was seated behind the desk in his quarters. In a chair across from him sat the dark-haired princess of Andara, ruler since the death of her father of the mightiest country of all Tarvius.

It was not so much the princess' request that bothered Rhon-Dee; it was an indefinable something in her eyes and her almost expressionless expression that he did not like.

"You question my wishes, Commander?" Ana-Bet said icily.

Rhon-Dee's jaw tightened and his eyes were suddenly angry. His voice came out with a harshness the girl had never heard there before. "We are alone here," he said. "I tell you now I do 'question your wishes!' I would not be following my duties as commander of this force if I failed to do so. The only man able to operate the machine already has his hands full setting up the delicate mechanism with which we expect to find some trace of Had-Sudol's missing ship. It requires two full days—possibly even longer—to get it adjusted. And now you want him taken off that job because of some idle whim? Do you plan to remain on this Novah-forsaken planet forever?"

She ignored the bitterness behind the man's question. "And if I *order* you to do it?"

Rhon-Dee's stony gaze did not waver. "Let me remind Her Highness that the machine she *orders* used on the captive can be extremely dangerous for the subject. The slightest mistake on the operator's part may rupture the blood vessels of the brain, causing death."

"I understand the technician is highly competent."

"He is also human!" Rhon- Dee snapped. "Right now his mind is concentrated on one job. Take him from it and force another in its place without giving him a day or two of rest—and the result might well be...unfortunate."

Abruptly Ana-Bet changed her tactics. "Just for an hour or so, Dee," she pleaded winningly. "Just so he can understand the rudiments of our language. You saw how he feared and mistrusted the translavox; perhaps if I could talk to him in words he could understand—perhaps then he will be able to tell us something about Had-Sudol."

A corner of Rhon-Dee's lips lifted in a smile that was not amused. "As you said earlier: he *is* a handsome beast..."

The princess' breath caught sharply—then she was out of her chair like a singed cat and a firm hand flashed in a sweeping arc that ended against the commander's left cheek.

For a long moment the two remained as if frozen—the girl half leaning across the desk, her eyes blazing, the man still seated, face expressionless, a red blotch staining the skin where the blow had landed.

Then almost casually he reached out and flipped one of the tiny switches set into the desk top.

"Have Technician Flav-Breom report to me immediately," he said.

CHAPTER SEVEN

AS HAD-SUDOL crumpled, his strength sapped by the savage blow, a feeling of hopelessness and despair welled up within him. So close to freedom—and now, even if he lived, it would mean a return to an eternity of empty days and nights, forever a prisoner.

But both he and his attackers reckoned without a girl in love—and therein lay their error.

Like a lioness bereft of her cubs, the daughter of Ulgo turned on the two warriors. From the belt of the nearest man she snatched a stone knife and plunged it to the hilt into his chest. Voicing a single choked scream he collapsed, and ere the second guard could recover his wits, the blood-stained flint caught him full in the throat, putting a grisly period to his startled cry.

And then the weapon was falling from the girl's nerveless grasp as, with a shudder of horror, she buried her face in her hands and dry convulsive sobs racked her slender body.

Comforting arms closed tenderly about her and she clung tightly to the still dazed Had-Sudol. He was a little amazed at the depths of the girl's grief, for her life in this savage world must have accustomed her to sudden and violent death.

Her first words made clear the reason for her distress. "Th-they were my friends," she choked. "All my life I have known them, talked, laughed, quarreled with them. And now I have *k-killed* them!"

The man made no effort to halt her words, but simply tightened his hold while the paroxysm of revulsion and self-reproach ran its course. When finally she grew calmer, he said, "There was no other way, Duleen; it was them or us. Come, we must go before others of the tribe find us— and them."

Carefully they crossed the ribbon of grass until the black wall of trees and jungle rose to confront them. From those Cimmerian depths came the restless rustle and sly stirrings of a night wind through tangled vegetation: sounds magnified by Had-Sudol's untrained ears into the pad of taloned paws and the scrape of sleek tawny hides against vines and bushes. Brave as the next man, confident of his own prowess, still he unconsciously moved closer to the girl at the thought of entering the forbidding territory.

To Duleen, this was familiar though undesirable ground. Turning left she skirted the forest edge, the man at her heels, until she reached a narrow break in the wall of trees.

"A game trail," she told Had-Sudol, whispering. "It turns and twists, but after a while it leads almost straight to the valley where Bulat said the shining rocks lay. There you will find your people."

Had-Sudol eyed the thin opening with misgivings. "We'd better get started," he said.

"I am staying here."

The man stiffened, bewildered. "Staying? But I thought—"

"Don't you see?" she said, a note of pleading in her voice. "We are not the same. A god can not mate with one who is not a god—any more than Conta, the lioness, can mate with Aka, the lightning…"

"But, Duleen," he pleaded. "I love you! I've loved you since the moment you stood there in the cave staring at me."

The darkness prevented him from seeing the tender smile that touched her lips, the involuntary lifting of her hands to touch him—a gesture she instantly suppressed.

"I know," she murmured. "And after a while, when you saw how different I was from the women of your people, you would begin to hate me. I could not bear that—I would rather lose you now than see that happen."

Time, Had-Sudol realized, was running out. At any moment relief might arrive for the guards, and discovery of those two lifeless bodies would bring a hornet's nest down upon the fugitives' heads.

And so he acted—acted as one of Ulgo's own warriors might have done. Before Duleen was aware of what he intended, Had-Sudol caught her roughly about the waist and flung her over one of his broad shoulders. More as a startled reaction to this unexpected violence, the girl began to kick and squirm; but Had-Sudol only tightened his hold and trotted through the opening in the jungle ramparts.

As the man and the woman he carried disappeared into that velvet well, Tarka, the panther, rose with casual silence from the concealing depths of verdure nearby and slunk cautiously along the game trail behind them.

*　*　*

FOR MORE than an hour now no word had been spoken in the small square white-walled room. Only the low steady hum of an electric motor and the deep regular breathing of the young giant on the table broke the silence.

Technician Flav-Breom, probably the greatest scientist in Tarvius' long history, glanced wearily at the chronometer strapped to one of his bony wrists. Another hour under the multiple and incredibly sensitive impulses of the Cephalscribe, Flav-Breom's greatest invention of a long and incredible list of inventions, and this half naked savage should be able both to understand and speak the language of his captors. Not fluently, of course; that would require a full eight to twelve hours. But enough so that he could understand and be understood.

The scrawny, half-bald little scientist glanced slyly at the princess Ana-Bet seated across the table from him, her chin resting in one palm, eyes intent on the sleeping man and the crown of electrodes and trailing wires he wore. Let her tell the commander fancy stories! He, Flav-Breom, knew the real reason she wanted the captive to know her language! A handsome face and rolling muscles—and every woman, princess or slave, swooned with ecstasy! But no use for a man to whisper words of love if they could not we understood...

"Is he all right, Flav-Breom?"

The little scientist nodded. "Of course. He sleeps like a child while the current engraves a memory of our tongue in his mind."

"But he has not moved since you began."

"How do you expect him to?" the technician said testily. "He's held to the table with straps *four* men could not break."

She looked relieved. "True. It's only that Rhon-Dee mentioned that the slightest mistake could kill him."

Flav-Breom was offended. "There can *be* no mistake while I'm here! Have you forgotten that I *made* the Cephalscribe, that it was I who discovered the prin—"

"I know," Ana-Bet said hastily. "None questions your wisdom, Flav-Breom. It's just that..." Her voice trailed off.

The technician was mollified. "See that?" he said, pointing to one of several dials set into the machine. "As long as the indicating needle does not reach the dial's red zone, nor slip back into the black zone, the subject is safe. And the moment he is ready and I cut the power, he will wake from his sleep and can talk with you. Another hour—two at the most—will be enough."

Again there was silence and the minutes passed slowly and monotonously. From beyond the closed door came the occasional slither of a sandaled foot along the metal corridor as a guard made his rounds. The barely audible purr of air-conditioning was so constant as to be unnoticed. The princess Ana-Bet remained on the white metal stool near the table, watching the swelling chest of the young giant, the magnificent shoulders, the banded layers of muscle sheathing his body. Clearly he made every other male of her knowledge suffer by comparison!

What would it be like, she wondered, to belong to such a man? To share his untamed life, to wander the jungle trails beside him, to spend the nights in his arms in some lofty cave? She felt her cheeks glow at such thoughts, but she could not put them from her.

And then there was Had-Sudol—what of him? It was he she wanted, he who held her heart. Yet she might as well face it: Had-Sudol was dead, for he could hardly have survived three years in this savage world. Was she truly in love with him—or with the memory of what he had meant to her while she was no more than a child? What if, instead, she took this splendid creature back to Andara—there to shape him, to build him into a nobleman of her court. She pictured him as he would appear in the green tunic of royalty. Somehow the prospect was less attractive than if he were still clad in the scrap of animal skin he now wore about his hips. Yes, it would be wrong to remove him from his natural surroundings, to transplant him among the hothouse blooms of her own world.

SO ENGROSSED was the princess in her thoughts that she did not hear the first flurry of battle as Ulgo and his hundred warriors launched their attack on the space ships.

Suddenly the hair-raising scream of a mortally wounded man tore apart the silence, and the pounding of running feet echoed in the corridor outside. Flav-Breom, eyes round with shock, bounded to his feet and threw open the door.

A wave of deep-tanned, half-naked bodies rolled along the corridor, sweeping before it a thin line of white-tunicked Andarans. Stone knives licked out and defenders fell before they could bring their deadly kodets into use. Those who did succeed in freeing those weapons from their belts had them battered from their hands before over-anxious fingers could press the firing buttons.

It was not that the warriors of Andara lacked courage or cool heads; it was simply that the attack had been so completely a surprise and the enemy so strange, that panic was at first unavoidable. The guards outside lay dead, sightless eyes staring at the night sky, arrow hafts protruding from their bodies—victims of as carefully planned and executed an ambush as even the Andarans themselves could have arranged. Thus the cavemen were able to enter the space ships in force before those within even dreamed that an attack was under way.

As Flav-Breom flung open the door, three of Ulgo's warriors spied him. With a savage snarl one lifted his spear and drove its point full into the little scientist's thin, unprotected chest. So tremendous was the power behind the thrust that the technician was lifted completely from his feet and thrown backward half across the room. Already dead, Flav-Breom's body plowed into the labyrinth of wires, tubes, coils and condensers that made up the Cephalscribe.

A soundless flash of blue flame caused the three cavemen to leap back from the doorway in alarm. Ana-Bet, breaking the chains of fear that held her, leaped forward and slammed the door. But as she fumbled for the lock, a brawny shoulder drove into the planks from the opposite side and she staggered back.

The first caveman swung up his knife to skewer the shrinking, terror-stricken princess. But one of his companions knocked the blade aside.

"Fool!" he spat. "There are better uses for a woman this shapely!"

One calloused hand shot out and caught the paralyzed girl by the wrist. Weakly she clawed at those steel fingers, but the burly brute only roared with laughter and drew her slowly, savoringly, into his arms.

The leering, evil face bent slowly toward her. She could see the lust distorted features, feel fingers groping at the neckline of her tunic, smell the fetid breath from his half-open, drooling lips. Her senses swam under the impact of pure horror and she felt her body grow limp.

It was then that Valar opened his eyes.

CHAPTER EIGHT

AFTER a couple of hundred feet, Had-Sudol failed to notice a bend in the trail and blundered squarely into the bole of a jungle patriarch. Half-stunned, he loosened his hold on the cave girl and she wriggled free.

Had Duleen made an attempt, then, she would have easily gotten away. Instead, she took the young man by an arm and drew him back to the game trail.

They stood there for several minutes while Had-Sudol's labored breathing slowed and the trembling of exhaustion left his limbs. When finally he felt he could trust his voice, he said:

"You could have run away just now, Duleen."

"I know," she said, almost inaudibly.

"Why didn't you?"

The darkness hid her tender smile. "Maybe I did not want to think of you wandering around in the jungle by yourself. Even if one of the big cats didn't get you, you'd never find your way to the valley of shining rocks. Where the forest is concerned, you are more helpless than a little child."

The words stung Had-Sudol's pride, although there was enough truth in them to keep him silent. Presently the girl said, "We are still too close to the caves. Let us go on for a while before we find a tree in which to remain until dawn."

Silently Had-Sudol turned and strode ahead, the girl following. As they moved on, the cave girl continued speaking, her voice barely more than a whisper.

"Walk lightly, using only the balls of your feet. Stop suddenly from time to time, straining your ears to learn if Kraga, the lion, or Conta, his mate, or Tarka, the panther, is stalking you. Be alert as you round each turn in the path, for it is in such places that Shanda, the leopard, waits for his prey."

This was jungle lore, straight from one who had been born while a lion roared over the body of its kill less than a hundred yards from the caves where her mother lay in labor, from one to whom the forest aisles were as familiar as the controls of a flier to Had-Sudol. And, as intelligent men always do, he listened when experience spoke— listened and remembered.

LESS THAN half an hour later the trail abruptly widened and became a small clearing covered by tangled grasses and the reed-lined banks of a tiny stream. Had-Sudol was all for plunging ahead and slaking his thirst, but the girl's hand at his arm held him back.

"It is the way of the great beasts to lie in wait among the river reeds," she told him. "Those who rush to water seldom live to cool their throats. We must wait a moment and make sure there is no danger."

They stood there, silent and unmoving as stone, listening, straining their eyes to pierce the gloom-shrouded banks of the brook. In Had-Sudol's right hand was a stout length of branch, which he had picked up earlier on the game trail.

It was while they stood there, all their attention on the possible danger ahead that Tarka, the panther, stepped delicately in the clearing not ten feet behind them.

Oddly enough, it was Had-Sudol who first sensed their peril. It seemed almost as if he was feeling a cold breath moving along the length of his spine—a sensation that cut through his preoccupation with making sure the way was open for quenching his thirst.

Almost without thinking, he turned his head sharply and glanced over his shoulder…and the blood seemed to freeze in his veins. Almost within arm's length, what little light there was picking out tooth and fang and gleaming eyes, was the savage head and tawny body of a giant cat.

Had-Sudol's involuntary gasp was enough to bring the girl about. She took one look at the fearsome head so near and a single sharp cry broke from her lips. And at that instant, Tarka, voicing a shrill scream, sprang toward his prey!

Whether he acted from bravery or the madness of fear, Had-Sudol never knew; but instead of trying to avoid the cat's charge, the man leaped blindly forward to meet it. As he came, he brought up high above his head the thick branch he carried, then swung it down in a vicious arc.

Tarka, having gauged his leap accurately, was totally unprepared for his intended victim's attempt to close with him. As a result, both talons and fangs were out of position for defense and there was no way for the giant cat to avoid the descending branch.

There came the dull crunch of splintered bone and, Tarka, skull caved in like a rotten fruit, seemed to halt in midair, then dropped in a limp heap in the center of the trail, dead where he fell. Had-Sudol stood there, slack-jawed with stupefaction, the splintered remnants of the branch still clutched tightly in his hand.

Duleen came up to him and said in an awed voice, "No warrior in all my father's tribe ever slew Tarka with nothing but a tree branch. Only a god could be that brave and that mighty!"

The young nobleman would have liked nothing better than to toss the handful of splinters aside with a careless gesture and put on a bored expression. But his peril was too recent, his relief too complete, for any such histrionics. He tried to speak but the words caught in his throat and he could do little more than gasp unintelligibly.

"Let's find that tree," he finally managed to say. "And the higher the better!"

VALAR, warrior of the tribe of Polex, opened his eyes to find himself half buried in the wreckage of what he last remembered as the thing that had plunged him into the black pit of unconsciousness.

His sharp eyes caught sight of the beautiful girl who had sat near him and watched intently while a scrawny elderly little man attached odd vines to his head. Now she was struggling furiously in the grasp of a leering caveman while two others watched in grinning approval. From beyond the room came the curses, groans and screams of men locked in mortal combat.

The three cavemen, Valar saw instantly, were members of some other tribe. This could only mean that they would kill him, once they caught sight of his bound and helpless body.

He bent his head and glanced at the broad leather straps confining his chest and arms. Before this he had made no serious attempt to test their strength, for always the watchful eyes of guards were on him. Drawing breath deeply into his lungs, he began to exert—steadily increasing pressure, forcing his body up and his sinewy arms out from his sides. The leather groaned, stretched slightly—and held. Without for a moment relaxing, Valar continued to press against his bonds, closing his mind to the pain as their edges began to cut into his skin.

Mighty were the muscles of Valar, but in those leather thongs was strength enough to hold back an elephant. Fortunately, however, the metal flanges to which they were secured proved to be comparatively weak. Under the enormous pressure two of them snapped almost simultaneously and the caveman was free.

And none too soon! Already one of the hulking intruders was moving toward him, knife in hand; a grimace of blood lust twisting his coarse features.

As a swimmer dives from a river bank, Valar shot from the high table. His catapulting body caught the other full in the belly, driving the air from his lungs in an audible *"whoosh"* and leaving him gasping and helpless on the floor.

Valar stopped quickly, hoping to wrest the stone knife from the fallen man's limp grasp. But the remaining pair, suddenly aware of their peril, leaped upon him before he could seize the weapon. Under their weight Valar fell to his knees as a flint blade struck full at his unprotected back.

Ana-Bet, hands pressed to her cheeks, eyes staring in stark horror, cried out in warning.

But Valar, veteran of many such battles, had anticipated the knife thrust. Even as he fell, he was twisting aside and the length of flint succeeded only in plowing a thin furrow in his side. Before the warrior of Ulgo could make a second attempt, strong fingers closed on his wrist and the bone snapped like a dry twig.

A howl of pain ripped from the man's throat and he rolled away as Valar leaped to his feet. The remaining warrior was no coward. Drawing his knife he flung himself upon the unarmed cave lord with all the silent ferocity of Kraga, the lion.

With the speed of light, Valar avoided the slashing blade, then lashed out with one rock-like fist backed by every ounce of weight he possessed. Bones splintered sickeningly, vertebrae snapped, and the lifeless clay of what had been one of Ulgo's finest fighting men crumpled to the floor.

VALAR SCOOPED up a stray knife and was bounding toward the open door, and freedom, when the sight of the girl huddled in one corner of the room brought him to a skidding halt.

As those blazing eyes fell upon her, a wave of faintness turned the princess' legs to water. Through a blur of tears she saw him hesitate, then turn and advance toward her, knife in hand, unmistakable menace in every line of that splendid body.

"No!" she gasped. "Don't—don't kill me!"

He stopped abruptly, and seeing this the girl gained courage, feeling that her plea was taking effect. "I will help you escape," she went on. "They will listen to me. They must, for—"

It was not her words that had stopped Valar; it was instead the startled awareness that he could now understand *what* she was saying. The reason for this phenomenon was unknown to him; in fact, he failed to wonder at it. But for some not clearly understood reason the fact that he could understand her made her of far more value to him than a possible hostage. What form that value might take he was not as yet aware, nor was there time for analysis.

Before she realized his intention, a tanned arm darted out and caught her about the waist. Wildly she struck out, but the cave youth ignored the blows and swung her lightly to his shoulder. Abandoning hope, the princess clung there as Valar turned and bolted through the door.

Some twenty or thirty feet down the corridor to his left was a hatchway open to the night air. Between him and that exit, however, were fully a dozen of Ulgo's half-naked warriors. Of the space ships' defenders there was no sign other than several torn corpses in blood-stained tunics strewn about the passageway.

Valar saw the enemy seconds before they caught sight of him and his lovely burden—and in that slim advantage lay his only chance for escape. So quickly did his agile brain seize upon it that to the princess there was no appreciable pause from the moment he entered the corridor until he was racing along it with great leaping strides.

The pound of naked feet was the first warning the cavemen were given; and as they whirled to face this new danger, Valar was already in their midst. Clutching the princess tightly, he laid about him with great sweeping blows of his free arm, upsetting men like saplings before a raging hurricane. Twice the knife in his hand drew blood: once slashing a naked chest from neck to groin, and again slashing a throat as its owner sought to impale Valar upon a spear.

So completely had Ulgo's men been taken by surprise, so devastating the attack by this lone warrior, that not even a hand was laid on him. Gaining the narrow hatch, he plunged through it and into the blackness beyond, before most of the survivors fully realized what had taken place.

MEANWHILE the tide had begun to turn in the battle raging in and around the row of space ships. So great had been the element of surprise that Ulgo's numerically inferior forces came very close to outright victory. Already three of the vessels were in the cavemen's hands, and only inability to make use of the stores of captured weapons kept them from turning the fight into a rout.

Rhon-Dee, commander of the expedition, had been forced to quit the flagship early in the fight, having used an emergency hatch in his cabin to make his escape. Blundering blindly through the night in an effort to find enough stragglers to form a counterattack, the officer barely managed to avoid death time and again. The searchlights he found to be battered into uselessness and their crews dead around them. It was this absence of illumination more than any other single factor, perhaps, that made his task nearly impossible. For the wild men of this planet were much at home in the darkness of jungle nights—a darkness beyond that of anything in the Andarans' experience—and they could recognize a foe and kill him while the visitors were still trying to make up their minds.

Finally Rhon-Dee managed to gather a few survivors together and equip them with kodets. With these flame pistols the men from Andara were able to turn favorably the fight going on in one of the ships, wiping out the cavemen there who had forced an entrance. From its store rooms, Rhon-Dee had several searchlights brought out into the open and set up in such a way that, at a signal from him, they would light up the area about the ships.

The commander, lips drawn into a hard straight line, made a final inspection before giving word for the lights to go on. He could hear the sobbing breathing of his men, the nervous shuffle of their feet in the long grass, and he sensed their burning hatred of an enemy like none they had ever faced before. In spite of the ordeal they were undergoing there was nothing of fear in them, and Rhon-Dee knew a quiet pride that this was so.

He crouched between two of the searchlights and checked the kodet in his hand. A last slow look around—then:

"Now!"

Instantly the clearing was flooded with light—light that seemed, after the intense darkness, to rival the radiance of the sun. At first the Andarans could do nothing more than blink helplessly while their eyes adjusted to the brilliance; then they began to make out the half-naked forms of Ulgo's men caught in the rays like insects on pins.

Thin rays of fire began to lance out from the kodets of Rhon-Dee's men and running figures fell to rise no more. Several made a valiant but completely useless attempt to charge the small group about the searchlights, and one by one they died long before they were close enough to throw their spears or release their arrows.

Suddenly Rhon-Dee grabbed the controls of the light nearest him and swung its rays to cover an open hatch in one of the ships. The powerful light picked out the figure of a giant caveman, a slender, softly rounded body in a green tunic across his shoulder.

As the beam found him, the huge figure whirled and raced with great bounding strides for the valley wall no more than a hundred yards away. The man next to Rhon-Dee growled a single word and leveled his kodet. Before he could press the firing pin the commander struck aside the weapon.

"Don't shoot, you fool!" he cried. "That's the princess he's holding!"

At his words, the men about him uttered choked cries of rage and without waiting for orders, two broke away and raced across the open ground in an effort to overtake Ana-Bet's abductor. But the flying figure left them behind as though they were rooted to the ground, and seconds later it had disappeared among the shadows of the overhanging cliffs.

Empty-handed, the two soldiers straggled back, feet dragging despondently. Rhon-Dee ground his teeth in rage as the full realization of this night's crowning blow came home to him.

"It is useless to try to find her before morning," he told the others dully. "Now we must win back our ships. But spare the lives of a few of these savages; we will force them to lead us to the one who has stolen Ana-Bet."

CHAPTER NINE

AS VALAR plunged into the shadows at the base of the valley rim, Ana-Bet, princess of Andara, felt her last shred of hope give way, and she resigned herself to only Novah knew what fate. As fascinating to her as this giant caveman was physically, she held no illusions of what being alone and helpless in his hands would mean. Either death would come quickly, or life would become a matter of waiting for an opportunity to do away with herself...

As the sheer valley wall rose before him, Valar never hesitated but swarmed up the rocky escarpment with an easy agility that left Ana-Bet breathless. Once over its rim he plunged ahead without pausing for breath, racing across the ribbon of grass there until he reached the first line of towering trees.

Into their branches he went—up and up until he was well above the cloaking tangle of vines and creepers; then he was moving once more in a horizontal plane, from tree to tree, while the stricken girl clung to him in mingled awe and terror and the glimmerings of reluctant admiration.

Ana-Bet lost all sense of time. It seemed that she was caught up in an insane nightmare filled with ghostly shadows and inky depths and a wild pattern of swaying boughs. Somewhere below was solid ground, but how far below she dared not think. Even her probable fate seemed no longer of importance; it was the now that mattered.

One moment her captor was swinging through the trees as though pursued by a thousand demons; and the next, he had halted abruptly on the high-flung branch of a jungle giant. Not ungently he lowered her to the rough bark near the tree bole and she sank down to a crouching position, holding desperately to the trunk.

Valar's keen eyes made out the taut expression on her face, and he smiled grimly. He wondered at the impulse that had made him keep this girl once his flight from the valley was successful. She had been no more than a hostage, a shield, then. But some impulse, some emotion, had kept him from tossing her aside once freedom was assured.

She was very beautiful he realized for the second time within a few hours. Far more beautiful than any girl of his tribe. Perhaps that was it. It was time he took a mate; all his friends had said that many times. True, this one was hardly a practical choice; she was more helpless than a child and, he could see, knew nothing of life in caves and jungle. If she was really a god, then gods were indeed a sorry lot and it was foolish to fear them. But it seemed likely that these were not gods. Had he not seen many of them torn to death by the savage fury of men like himself?

Yes, she would be his mate. He would like having her as his mate. She was soft and rounded and her hair was like a jungle night filled with the smell of flowers. He would be very gentle with her lest he bruise the white perfection of her; and he would bring the choicest foods for her to eat and teach her the duties of cave women. It was right that the most beautiful girl in all the world should be the mate of the world's mightiest warrior!

HE WATCHED her huddling there, clinging to the tree, and a wave of tenderness swept through him. He put out a hand and touched her hair gently, marveling at its silken texture. He let the fingers slide lingeringly down until they brushed gently against her throat.

Slender, sharp-tipped fingers lashed out and slashed him violently across his cheek. The nails bit deep, almost plunging the caveman into the black depths below.

So this was how she returned his caress! Voicing a low growl, he caught her by the shoulder as she made a pathetic attempt to scramble away. Roughly he dragged her close, but the hand raised to cuff her into submission never fell.

Instead, Valar swept the startled girl tight against his naked chest and covered her lips with kisses.

For a moment, the princess fought back with a silent intensity born of outraged dignity and fear. But only for a moment. Then her arms came up and closed lingeringly about his neck as with closed eyes she responded to the demands of those burning lips...

And then Ana-Bet, princess of Andara, tore herself from the wild man's arms and buried her shame-flushed face in her hands.

What was happening to her? she thought dazedly. Never before had she kissed any man—not even Had-Sudol—in the way that she had this—this savage! She could feel the pounding of her heart—and she knew it was not the pounding of fear but that of another emotion far, far different.

As for Valar—he was no less confused. The ways of a woman were strange to him—and becoming steadily stranger. Seconds ago she had made his senses reel with the ardency of her response to his kisses; now she was as though a world removed.

Hesitantly he reached out to touch her arm, only to have her jerk away as though he was Cretah, the hyena.

"No!" The tone of utter loathing in her voice was for herself far more than for him, but the man could not know that. "No! Don't touch me!"

"I want to touch you," he said simply. "You are mine. You shall come with me to the caves of Polex and we will be together always."

Ana-Bet's head came up furiously. "You—you animal! I hate you! Take me back where you found me or Rhon-Dee and his men will hunt you down and kill you like the beast you are!"

A VAGRANT ray of Mua, the moon, filtered through the foliage overhead, picking out the calm dignity in the caveman's handsome face, and the girl was stricken into shamed silence. Impulsively she laid a hand softly on one of his bronzed forearms.

"I didn't mean that, Valar," she whispered. "But I—I can't stay with you. Take me back."

For a long time the man stared at her without speaking, his face empty of expression. Then he shook his head, almost violently.

"No. When Oru comes again, I will take you to the caves of my people. You are mine—and what is mine I keep."

Rising, he picked her up with unexpected gentleness and placed her in a sitting position within a fork of a wide branch. "It is time we slept," he said. "In the morning I will take you to the tribe of Polex."

Before she could voice a protest, he left her—swinging to a branch directly over, where he was hidden among the leaves. The bough swayed gently for a moment, then was still; and though twice she called out to him, there was no response.

Her relief at being free, even temporarily, of Valar's disturbing presence was tempered by an unreasoning pique that he could so calmly leave her at all. She thought of descending to the ground while the caveman slept and finding her way back to the encampment. But in what direction the valley lay was by now pure guesswork; and when, a little later, a lion roared somewhere below she gave up the idea hurriedly.

The chill of a jungle night began to make itself felt. She knew she would never be able to sleep here, cramped and cold and forced to cling to a swaying branch.

Even as the thought came, her head had begun to nod. Seconds later she was sound asleep.

CHAPTER TEN

HARDLY had the first flush of dawn stained the eastern horizon than the Andaran encampment boiled with activity. Graves were dug to receive those honored dead who had come millions of miles across space to find a final resting place. The bodies of Ulgo's defeated horde were dragged out and burned in the valley's center, lest the corpses attract the jungle beasts and endanger the living.

But it was near the flagship that activity was heaviest. A hundred heavily armed fighting men, the pick of Andara's forces, began to form a double line while awaiting the order to march forth in search of the missing princess. Their faces were grim and intent, their voices silent, their actions purposeful. Ana-Bet, for all her imperious manner and quick tongue, was the darling of her country's warriors and there were few among them who would not have willingly given his life for her safe return.

Now came the lean and muscular Rhon-Dee, commander of the fleet, his striking, hawk-like face set in bleak lines. With him, between two guards, was the only captive taken during the night's battle: a hulking sullen-faced caveman, arms bound, a lead-rope about his thick neck.

After a brief word to the men, Rhon-Dee moved to the column's head, accompanied by the caveman and his guards. The order to march was given and the twin line moved briskly across the valley to the cliffside. Up the face of living rock went the hundred warriors, making hard work of it, for the ascent would have taxed the abilities of a mountain goat. When all were assembled at the upper edge, the captive managed to pick up Valar's spoor among the grasses, and the column followed him to the jungle's edge.

Here, at the base of a towering tree, their guide stopped and scratched his head in obvious helplessness. By signs he managed to convey that the quarry had taken to the trees at this point—a route he was unable to follow. Judging from his gestures, a caveman who used the highway usually reserved for little Tola, the monkey, was something new in his experience and he seemed more than slightly impressed.

After consulting with his lieutenants, Rhon-Dee decided to lead his men along a game trail nearby, that followed a wavering course into the jungle. It was entirely possible they would be led in an altogether different direction by doing so, but there seemed no alternative.

A few minutes later the last of the rescue party disappeared into the gloomy sea of plant life.

* * *

ORU, THE SUN, was half above the horizon to the east when Ana-Bet opened her eyes. For a moment she could not recall where she was; then remembrance of last night's events flooded back and she rose shakily to her feet on the wide branch.

A soft sound behind her brought the girl around quickly. Standing there, a quizzical smile bending his firm lips, was Valar, his arms filled with succulent fruits.

They ate in silence for a while before Ana-Bet looked up and surprised him staring at her. "Take me back to my people, Valar," she said. "I do not...love you. I could never love any man who took me by force."

He shrugged and his fine eyes were shadowed with sadness. "No," he said tonelessly. "You belong to me."

"Would you want a girl who hates you?"

"Your words say you hate me," he replied. "But when your lips are against mine, they say something else."

Two angry spots of color burned in her cheeks. "I was frightened. I didn't know— It meant nothing. Can't you understand that it...meant nothing?"

Instead of replying, Valar tossed aside the rind of the fruit he had been gnawing and rose to his feet. "Oru is well into the sky," he said. "We must reach the caves before the day draws too hot for travel."

The girl did not move. "Then you will not take me back?"

She might as well not have spoken. He extended his hand to help her rise and said, "Come."

Instead of traveling through the trees as on the night before, Valar carried her down through the branches until he paused directly above a narrow game trail. After making sure no danger lurked in the immediate vicinity, the caveman dropped lightly to the dusty path and lowered his burden to her feet. "Let us walk for a while," he said.

Ana-Bet glanced nervously at the tangled walls of foliage on either side of the trail. "What if we meet one of the horrible beasts Rhon-Dee says are to be found on this world?"

One corner of Valar's mouth quirked and he patted the knife at his waist. "Soon you will learn that your mate is the greatest fighter in all the world. With no more than a knife I have slain Kraga, the lion! No other man has done that. No other man can travel through the trees as I do; no other man can find game by means of his nose alone. I am the greatest hunter, the mightiest fighter who ever lived!"

"You are also," the princess said acidly, "the greatest boaster who ever *will* live!"

But she caught herself smiling as she said it. How like a little boy this wild man was! Perhaps all primitive people were given to swaggering and boasting, she thought, and I shall have to get used to it.

For the better part of an hour they moved along the path, Valar holding back his swinging, springy gait to keep from leaving the girl behind. Most of the way he walked ahead, eyes and nose alert, his right hand never far from the knife at his belt.

SUDDENLY Valar froze to a halt almost in mid-stride, his head lifted alertly and the thin line of his nostrils quivered. To Ana-Bet it was almost as though his ears twitched forward like those of an animal, and although she strained her ears to the utmost she could hear nothing beyond the already familiar rustle of foliage and hum of insects, which made up the customary jungle background.

Valar made a vague sound deep in his throat. Taking the wondering girl by an arm, he left the trail and slipped behind a curtain of vines and leaves. Ana-Bet was on the point of demanding an explanation but he clapped a palm across her lips and shook his head in warning.

They had not long to wait. The princess caught a murmur of voices first, followed by the sound of feet against bare earth. And then she saw what at first she thought were two cave people: a lovely girl in the barely adequate pelt of some animal, and a man wearing a loin cloth of the same material. They drew nearer, until she could almost reach out and touch them.

It was then that Ana-Bet, princess of far-off Andara, forgot all caution in the thrill of amazed recognition.

"Had-Sudol!" she screamed; and before even Valar's lightning-like reflexes could act, she was through the curtain of foliage and had thrown herself into the arms of the tall figure on the trail.

The young nobleman's jaw dropped until it almost unhinged as he recognized the girl. "B-Bet!" he stammered. "What in Novah's name are—"

He broke off in alarm as a second figure crashed into the open, and he saw the rage-distorted features of a magnificent caveman bearing down upon him. He pushed aside the princess and threw one arm up in a futile attempt at defense. A soundless flash of pain seemed to split his head into flaming bits, the ground spun up to meet him and the blackness of unconsciousness poured into his brain.

Valar, deep in the throes of jealousy, leaped forward to finish the kill. But as quickly as he moved, another was even quicker.

Something that seemed all blonde hair, fury and fingernails exploded full in his face, forcing him to back away a step or risk losing an eye. Duleen, untamed daughter of a savage chief, had come to the aid of the man she loved.

Like a man annoyed by an overzealous mosquito, Valar snaked out an arm, caught the raging, spitting girl about the waist and casually threw her, twisting and turning in mid-air, into a tangle of bushes thirty feet away. She made a convulsive effort to rise, but the breath was gone from her lungs and she sank back gasping for air.

Again the caveman reached for his victim—and again he was interrupted. Between him and the senseless nobleman of Andara stood Ana-Bet, straight as an arrow, her dark eyes flashing.

"Let him alone!" she cried. "Haven't you hurt him enough?"

But Valar, the memory of the girl he loved in the arms of another still burning in his mind, thrust her roughly aside. As those steel fingers closed on Had-Sudol's throat, Ana-Bet made one last effort to save his life.

"Wait, Valar!" she pleaded. "Leave him unharmed and I will be your mate!"

THE CAVEMAN'S grip slackened and he turned his head to stare up at her, puzzled and suspicious. "You belong to me now," he growled. "I have told you that you are to be my mate."

"I will be no man's mate unless I want to be," she said, almost whispering. "Yes, you can take me coldly and against my will. But if you do, I will kill you someday. There will come a time when you must sleep, when you cannot watch me. Then I will kill you—with a knife, with a rock, perhaps with a push as you stand near the edge of a cliff. But someday my chance will come!"

Valar's keen mind digested the words and a faint smile of respect and admiration for this proud woman brushed his lips. Not for a moment did he question that she would do exactly as she said.

"And if I do not kill him?"

Her face crimsoned but her gaze never wavered. "Then I will...belong to you in the way you want me to."

The caveman's eyes flickered from her to the man on the ground and back to her again. "Why are you ready to do this for him?" he growled. "What is he to you?"

"He is from my world, Valar," she said. "He came here long ago—and when he did not return we came in the ships you saw to hunt for him."

"What is he to you?" the cave lord repeated.

"Does that matter—now?"

The fingers left the unconscious man's throat and Valar stood erect. "For what you promise, I will not kill him." He held out a hand to her. "Come."

Without hesitation, head proudly lifted and shoulders squared, Ana-Bet went to him. Valar swung her easily into his arms, then turned and vaulted into the overhanging branches of a nearby tree...

CHAPTER ELEVEN

ONCE SHE regained her breath and the mists of pain lifted, Duleen was able to stagger weakly to her feet.

Except for the limp body of Had-Sudol the trail was empty.

Fearfully she knelt in the dust beside the young Andaran. Blood from one nostril had stained the angle of his jaw and his cheeks seemed pale and drawn. But his bronzed chest rose and fell under even breathing and Duleen's heart swelled with relief and thanksgiving.

She sat there for what appeared to be hours, cradling his head in her arms, until finally his eyes opened slowly and he stared blankly up at her.

"Duleen," he muttered. "What—?"

And then he remembered and his eyes were no longer blank, but cold with something that was beyond anger. "Where is she?" he said hoarsely. "What has he done to her?"

Roughly, without waiting for an answer, he pushed away her arms and tried to rise. But not until the third attempt, with Duleen's help, was he successful. He swayed there in the path, his eyes searching and a little wild. "Where is she?" he said again.

It was then that something seemed to die inside the cave girl. "He took her," she said dully. "I saw him take her in his arms and leap into a tree."

Had-Sudol weaved unsteadily to the tree she indicated and peered upward through the mazes of foliage there.

"He's gone," he said, turning to her. "Who is he? Where would he take her?"

"I never saw him before," the girl said. "I cannot say where he took her. Unless..."

His hands bit into her shoulders. "Unless what?"

She made no attempt to shake off his grasp. "I have heard it said that another tribe has its caves in that direction." She pointed toward the north. "They do not come into the hunting grounds of my father's people, nor do we go to theirs."

"You think he is from that tribe?"

"It could be so."

Had-Sudol's hands fell from her shoulders and he bit his lips, thinking. "This trail forked back there aways," he said presently. "Remember? The other branch led in the direction you say this tribe has its caves. I'm going to try it!"

She was watching him through eyes that had narrowed slightly. "Why must you do that?" she asked.

His frown said that the question was ridiculous. "You don't think I'd leave her in the hands of that—that *buliff*, do you?"

Duleen had no idea what a buliff was, but his tone told her that to him there was nothing more despicable. "She means so much to you?"

It was more statement than question. But Had-Sudol, in his impatience to be gone, was no longer listening. It was in his silence that Duleen read her answer—and believed it to be the true one. She did not know—she could not know—that the man's determination to rescue the princess Ana-Bet was not motivated by love—at least not the love a man holds for the one woman of his choice. To Had-Sudol, Ana-Bet was a symbol: the synthesis of the land of his fathers and their fathers for countless generations, of the country he loved. Like any soldier, he would die for Ana-Bet; for Ana-Bet *was* Andara.

He pointed ahead along the trail. "Try to find the valley where my people are. They will look after you until I return."

He turned and started back. Duleen called out, "Wait! I am going with you!"

He shook his head impatiently. "What good would that do? I'd only have to look after you, too."

"You do not know the ways of the cave people as I do," she told him. "You will need all the cunning of both of us to take your woman away from an entire tribe."

It made sense; Had-Sudol was forced to admit. And come to think of it, this girl could probably do a much better job of taking care of herself than he could—at least as far as life in this savage world was concerned.

"All right," he said. "Come on, then."

BY THE time Had-Sudol and Duleen reached the vicinity of the caves of Polex, nightfall was hardly more than an hour away. Cautiously they crouched down behind a curtain of foliage high among the branches of a forest giant and peered out at the scene below.

It was but little different from what both of them had seen many times before while with Ulgo's people. What might have been the same naked children, darted at play among the toiling women and lolling warriors. At the spring a knot of the women were filling cooking pots for the evening meal, and in the sunniest spot to be found, the old men of the tribe warmed their aged bones and spoke presumably wise words to one another.

Had-Sudol was in a fever of impatience. For hours he had been forced to lay up through the heat of mid-day instead of pushing on to his goal. But Duleen, far more familiar with the laws of jungle survival, would not permit it. She had pointed out that nothing could be done toward rescuing the princess during the light of day; that any attempt to do so was almost hopeless at best without their being completely exhausted before they even started. Only the very strong or the very foolish went running about during the terrible enervating heat of mid-day, and she had been adamant that they avoid doing so.

Had-Sudol's eyes ceased to dart about the clearing below and disappointment clouded his features. "I don't see her," he said.

Duleen's heart contracted painfully at the panic in his tone. How he must love this black-haired girl of his own kind! With an effort she kept the hurt from betraying itself as she spoke.

"She is there. In one of the caves, probably."

Relief and doubt struggled in his expression. "How can you tell?" he said eagerly.

"Look," she replied, pointing. "There—just within the clearing's edge, to the right of the cliff. That warrior who talks to the man with the skin of Kraga, the lion, about his hips."

Had-Sudol's eyes followed her directions and he stiffened. "It's he! The one who took her!"

"Even had I not seen him," Duleen said calmly, "I would know they are here. Watch the women at the spring. See how they talk and laugh excitedly among themselves while they glance often at the caves. It is the way of women when they speak of a warrior and his new mate."

"He shall never have her," Had-Sudol said grimly, so low that Duleen barely made out the words. For an instant it seemed to the girl that he was on the point of leaping from the branch to charge the entire tribe, and she placed a quieting hand on his tense arm.

"How can we learn in which cave she's held?" he said.

Duleen considered the question thoughtfully. "We must watch to see which cave he enters," she said finally. "There is a chance that she will come out to eat with him beside the cooking fires when Oru is gone from the sky. But it is not likely she will want to so soon."

THE MAN caught the meaning in those last words and his fingers clenched helplessly. "What can I do?" he burst out. "What can I *do?*"

"Nothing—now. Nothing but wait until the tribe sleeps—"

A horrible thought flashed through the young nobleman's brain. "But by then it may be too late! He may have—may have—"

He broke off, flushing, hating even to put the thought into words, to find the girl staring at him with puzzled eyes.

"Too late?" she repeated. "He would not bring her so far only to kill her."

Had-Sudol did not enlarge on the subject. Despite the three years he had spent among the cave people, he knew next to nothing of either their mores or their morals. But he did know that the princess Ana-Bet was in the hands of a wild savage who could not fail to be aroused by her loveliness of face and form.

Dusk began to deepen in the clearing, and Had-Sudol suffered the tortures of the damned waiting for Ana-Bet's captor to give some indication of which of the caves was his. Another warrior had joined the first two by now and some sort of heated discussion seemed to be going on. This third warrior had only just arrived from the jungle and immediately sought out the chief.

Finally, when the light was so dim that the Andaran was barely able to distinguish his man, the brawny cave lord turned, crossed the clearing with springy steps and entered one of the dark openings in the lower tier of caves dotting the cliffside.

He was out again, almost at once, carrying a heavy spear. About his shoulders were the coils of a grass rope, a quiver of arrows and bow of black wood. Standing there, shoulders squared and head thrown back, the gray cliff rising above him, he might have been some dusky-skinned forest god from the dawn of Time.

He raised his voice in a kind of chanting shout that carried clearly to the couple in the tree. In response, warriors began to cluster around him while women hurried into the caves, then reappeared with weapons, which they handed to their men.

Duleen explained what was taking place. "A returning hunter caught sight of some sort of game—just what I don't know. A hunting party is forming to go after it, and the chances are fair that they may not return until late. You are lucky indeed, Had-Sudol; for the fewer warriors there are about, the greater your chances of freeing your woman."

He was on the point of explaining that Ana-Bet was not "his woman," when a fresh burst of activity interrupted him. The hunting party was complete now—over thirty strong—and amidst a hubbub of excitement from women and children, it set out across the circle of open ground for the game trail entrance into the jungle.

Moments after the men disappeared from view, the utter darkness of night plunged the clearing into blackness, and soon cooking fires began to dot the scene. The remainder of the tribe of Polex gathered about the flames and the feasting began.

Had-Sudol was suddenly aware of Duleen's hand on his arm. He looked around and was barely able to make out the white oval of her face near his own.

"They will stay about the fires for hours," she said tautly. "It is the custom when hunters go out so late. The caves will be deserted now—unwatched; the girl, alone."

Had-Sudol's pulse leaped. "Of course! Later, when the tribe sleeps, the guards would be a problem." He rose to his feet on the branch. "Wait for me here, Duleen. When I have freed the princess I will come back for you."

"May the gods watch over you," she said quietly, and for a second Had-Sudol thought he heard a sob behind the words.

UPON REACHING the base of the tree, Had-Sudol began a slow circling at the outer edge of the clearing, working his way toward the point where the encroaching forest and jungle met the cliffside a hundred yards or so below the caves of Polex. He kept within the fringes of vegetation, moving with all the stealth at his command, for he had no idea whether or not guards were stationed at the periphery of open ground in anticipation of just some such enemy patrol action.

But for a long time no foe had attacked these cave people and safeguards had been gradually relaxed. So it was that the young Andaran, totally inexperienced though he was in this type of campaign, found it comparatively easy to reach the juncture of cliff and jungle hardly more than a stone's throw from the cave entrances.

By the flickering light of cooking fires he counted off those gaping shadowy holes nearest the escarpment's base. The fifth from this end—that was it! Or was it the sixth? Somehow from this new perspective things looked totally different. For one thing the first row of caves was higher from the ground than he had imagined. Fifteen feet— perhaps even more—would have to be scaled before he could reach Ana-Bet.

Carefully he planned each move he must make, each step he must take along the way, trying to anticipate every danger that could possibly arise. For him to cross those hundred yards by stealth would be sheer suicide. Boldness must be the keystone of his plan. He was sharply aware that he was completely unarmed. What wouldn't he have given for just one small kodet! Even a stone knife such as these wild men used would have been welcome.

The realization came that he must delay no longer. And so, calling silently to his god for protection, Had-Sudol stepped leisurely into the open and began to stroll casually along the edge of the towering cliff toward the first line of caves.

The first few strides were easy enough; but a feeling of suspense and strain began to rise in him from that moment on. It seemed that he was moving through an area of light a hundred times more brilliant than could be created by a score of powerful spotlights. Surely every hair on his body would be perfectly visible to the cave people about the fires. His skin seemed to crawl under the impact of innumerable eyes. A shiver ran along his legs and shook his knees until he was ready to swear they were pounding together like beaten gongs.

With an attempt at casualness that required superhuman effort, he swung his eyes to the nearest group of humans...and felt his senses reel. Although his judgment shouted that they were fully sixty feet away, he could have sworn that an outstretched hand from anyone of them could have grabbed his shoulder.

Doggedly he plodded on, heart pounding as though trying to leap from his chest. The first fire was behind him, now the second, now the thir—

A BULKY caveman, the half-gnawed rib of Tao, the deer, protruding from his gnarled fist, turned away from the third fire and stared straight at Had-Sudol. He took a step or two toward the young nobleman and called out something to him, waving the bone for emphasis.

Up and down Had-Sudol's legs continued, knees flexing and straightening, body pulled forward by reflex action alone. Even fear was gone from him now; there was only a numbness imparted by a mind that refused to endure further the awful suspense.

The man at the fire hesitated, shrugged slightly and turned back to the fire...and to Had-Sudol's ears his own sigh of relief was as loud as a raging hurricane.

The fourth fire drifted past not more than fifty feet to his left, then the fifth—and he was standing directly below the cave he had decided earlier housed the captive Ana-Bet. He slowed to a halt even as his eyes were darting across the fifteen feet of rock between the ground and the hole in the cliff. He made out the outcroppings of living rock that made up the necessary hand—and foot—holds used to reach the caves. It would be fairly simple for any reasonably agile person to make use of them.

At this point his danger, no matter how great before, must become even greater. Should he be seen entering the cave of a warrior who the entire tribe knew was away, suspicion would become outright alarm and they would be down on his head like a swarm of insects.

Up the side of the cliff went Had-Sudol, his movements sure and swift as if he had spent a lifetime doing nothing else. At any moment he expected to hear a yell of alarm from behind him, followed by the thunder of running feet. But neither happened and he passed into the Cimmerian depths of the cave.

After a few steps—only just enough to be sure he was out of sight from the clearing—he stopped and flattened himself against one of the side walls. His labored breathing eased and he strained his ears to listen, seeking to shut out the babble of voices from outside.

At first he could hear nothing else; then, so faintly he could not be sure, he caught the sounds of soft breathing in the blackness beyond.

The hairs lifted along Had-Sudol's neck. Stealthily he began to move toward the sound, careful to avoid striking any loose object that might betray him.

The sound of breathing was more audible now, and suddenly his bare toes scraped lightly against the soft warmth of human skin.

Had-Sudol froze, expecting to hear a shout of alarm, a scream of fear—anything. But the slow even sound went on and his nerves ceased their twitching.

With all the care of a man fondling a bubble, the young Andaran extended a hand toward the sleeper. In this pit of blackness his eyes were useless; he must get his information through the sense of touch alone.

Warm breath moved against his fingers and he was acutely aware of the animal heat of the invisible body inches from where he now crouched. His hand drifted on, then settled like a drifting leaf…and encountered the soft fragrant profusion of a woman's hair.

Was it Ana-Bet's hair or that of some cave woman? The answer could mean the difference between life and death for him. All speculation was useless, even dangerous; he must act—and act now.

ALMOST BRUTALLY he clapped the palm of one hand across the sleeping woman's mouth; and as she awoke and strained upward against his hold, he whispered frantically in an unseen ear: "Bet! It is I—Had-Sudol! For the love of Novah don't move! Don't make a sound!"

The straining body relaxed and fell back so abruptly that he feared the girl had fainted. Still not entirely sure that she was Ana-Bet, he lifted his muffling hand slightly, ready to slap it back against the girl's lips should she attempt to scream.

Instead of a cry for help, however, he heard words in a breathless whisper: "Had-Sudol! How— Where—"

"Shhhh," he hissed. "We're getting out of here—I hope! But you've got to listen closely and do exactly as I tell you. One slip, one little move that's out of place, and we're both lost!"

Now fully awake, Ana-Bet found her mind churning with tangled emotions. To escape, to return to her own people—the thought was intoxicating! Yet with it came, unbidden, the memory of Valar holding her in his arms and smiling down at her back there in the jungle. His face, handsome and proud and intelligent, seemed to form before her, and it was almost as though she could feel the warmth of his muscular body close to her own...

Had-Sudol was urging her to her feet. "They're at the fires," he was saying, his voice so low she was barely able to make out the words. "I'll go first, but you must stay very close. When we reach the ground, we'll stroll together along the side of the cliff, like two young lovers who want to be alone. If anyone calls to us, we'll be much too interested in each other to hear. Can you do this, Bet? Can you act that way when your legs are trying to run and you dare not let them?"

"I-I think so," she breathed. "But—but—"

Something in her voice—a doubt, a reluctance—snagged his breathing with sudden horror. "I wasn't too late, my princess? He didn't—he didn't dare to—to—"

For a moment she had no idea what he was trying to say. Then understanding brought an invisible color to her cheeks and she choked down what threatened to be a gale of almost hysterical laughter.

"No, Had-Sudol," she said gravely. "It is not too late." And she wondered if the unseemly note of regret in her voice was audible.

At the cave's entrance, Had-Sudol paused and glanced searchingly about the clearing. There was no change; the fires burned brightly and the cave people were still around them, eating, talking and laughing.

The young nobleman, his heart trying to push his tongue aside, lowered himself over the narrow ledge and began the short descent. The princess followed close behind him and a moment later they were standing together on level ground.

Side by side, arms about each other's waists as befitted young lovers, they began to walk slowly toward the distant jungle. To them both the wall of trees appeared miles away and seemed to recede in spite of their efforts to cut down the gap of open ground.

AS THEY moved on, Had-Sudol kept up a running barrage of whispered words of comfort and encouragement, seeking to lessen the girl's nervousness. But Ana-Bet needed no such help; she was aware of no fear or strain.

Not until they were nearly two thirds of the way to safety did their bubble of hope burst—and it did so with a suddenness that left them both momentarily paralyzed, unable to move.

A shout of anger and alarm burst simultaneously from the throats of several men about the nearest fire, and five warriors, spears lifted threateningly, came racing toward them. And in that instant of paralysis Had-Sudol realized what had betrayed them.

The princess Ana-Bet was wearing a tunic instead of the length of animal skin common among the cave people!

A wave of anger at his own stupidity shook Had-Sudol, but it was too late now for self-condemnation.

"*Run!*" he shouted, and seizing the girl by one arm, plunged for the now nearby jungle with all the speed he could muster.

The distance to safety narrowed swiftly, but far swifter came the enraged pursuers. The thud of racing feet grew loud—louder—until it beat in the ears of the Andarans…and the haven of growing things was still yards away.

All hope left Had-Sudol as he realized the distance was too great. Only one thing could save the princess—and the princess alone!

With a savage thrust of his arm he literally threw the girl toward the spur of jungle, then wheeled abruptly and, with nothing but his two clenched fists, faced the warriors of Polex.

So unexpected was the maneuver, so completely without fear this lone man's bearing, that the first line of cavemen skidded to a sudden and involuntary halt. But only for a moment. Spear arms flashed back ready to hurl flint-tipped death at this madman who dared face overwhelming odds...and then the lone warrior was alone no longer!

From the depths of the jungle suddenly sprang a second figure, which crossed the distance between with flashing strides, and hurled itself upon the enemy. A short heavy branch in the form of a bludgeon rose and fell over and over in swift blows that sent two of them senseless to the ground.

But there could be only one outcome—and it came at once. Three flint-tipped lengths of wood licked out and tore into living flesh and the slender figure sank silently to earth.

"Duleen!" The word burst forth from the lungs of Had-Sudol in a sobbing scream, and he threw himself wildly upon the enemy, fists swinging with the blind fury of utter madness.

To Ana-Bet, princess of Andara, watching with horrified eyes from the edge of the forest, it seemed almost as if the young nobleman opened his arms to welcome Death's coming embrace. Cold flint tore into him and he fell as a great trees falls, full across the lifeless body of the girl he loved—the girl who preferred death to a life without him.

Lit by the blood-red fires, filled with shifting shadows under the wavering flames, the scene burned itself forever in the mind of Andara's princess. Then blindly she turned away and ran, sobbing and shivering uncontrollably, toward the game trail.

CHAPTER TWELVE

HOW LONG she raced along that dusty ribbon, panting and weeping, Ana-Bet never knew. Time and again she stumbled and fell, only to rise again and stagger on through the blackness of the jungle night. Her tunic ripped and tore under the raking bite of thorn-studded vines and bushes; her hair was tangled and filled with bits of vegetation, her legs bled from a score of scratches criss-crossing her soft skin.

Finally she could go no further and heedless of the possible danger from prowling meat-eaters, she sank to the ground and lay there waiting for her heart to cease its mad pounding or stop altogether—she cared not which.

And it was there, huddled in a pitiful heap, that Rhon-Dee and his column of Andaran fighting men found her. Tenderly she was lifted up and borne back through the jungle to the valley where lay the ships of Andara. Men skilled in the arts of healing bathed away the evidence of her ordeal, bound up her wounds and placed her between cool sheets. And not once during all this did Ana-Bet's eyes open, and not once did she realize what was taking place...

IT WAS mid-afternoon. In the cabin of the flagship the princess Ana-Bet sat in a comfortable chair staring out listlessly at the valley wall and the heavy growth of trees and bushes masking its base.

For the past several hours preparations for leaving this untamed planet had been under way. Seated at his desk across from the princess, Rhon-Dee had issued a steady stream of orders to officers, crew members and soldiers. All equipment was now back on board and hatches were being tightened.

The muted roar of engines was beginning to fill the valley outside with a sound like distant thunder. Rhon-Dee finished computations on a huge chart spread across his desk and leaned back rolling the stylus between fingers that, as he stared at the lovely sad-faced girl in the chair, were none too steady.

"We wait," he said formally, "only Her Highness' command."

She did not even turn her eyes to look at him. "Give the order, Dee," she said tonelessly. "Let us get off this accursed world and never come back. All of it is not worth even one of the lives it has taken from us."

"At once," the man said, and reached for the small lever that would permit his order to take off to reach the captains in charge of the other ships.

Before he reached it, however, Ana-Bet's voice, suddenly alive with excitement and some other emotion he could not immediately classify, stopped his hand.

"Wait, Rhon-Dee! There is something—someone— He has come back!"

The commander left his chair hurriedly and joined her in front of the port hole. He saw the tall, broad shouldered figure of the caveman whom he had last seen bearing the princess into the jungle. He was standing in the open only a few feet from the base of a lofty tree, naked except for the loin cloth at his hips, his leonine head lifted with all the unconscious dignity of a lion. An idle breeze stirred the long thick hair on his head and the bright sun picked out the smooth swell of muscles beneath bronzed skin.

"Open a hatch, Dee," the girl said in a voice that was none too steady.

"Open a—?" Rhon-Dee's jaw dropped. "In Novah's name, *why*? Surely you're not going to let that—that *freak* come aboard?"

"And why not?" she blazed, facing him angrily. "I can induce him to come with us to Andara." Her voice softened abruptly. "You see, Rhon-Dee, he loves me—and I love him!"

The commander straightened as though she had struck him. "Are you mad? Love that—that— I would sooner see you dead!"

Her chin lifted imperiously and her eyes were cold. "You will do as I say or find yourself in irons within minutes!"

Rhon-Dee's eyes veiled and he took a deep unsteady breath. "As Her Highness commands," he said thickly and slid a finger beneath the edge of his desk. There was the sound of grinding gears and a section of the cabin wall swung slowly open.

Without a backward glance Ana-Bet was through it and dropped lightly to the long grass of the valley floor. On winged feet she raced across the open ground toward the lone figure near the towering cliff and her heart raced in tempo with her steps.

Suddenly the muffled beat of engines behind her changed to a whining scream, and she whirled about just in time to see the great space ships lift, one after another, into the clear air. A scream of fear rose to her lips as she realized that she was being marooned here on this untamed planet. This, then, was Rhon-Dee's answer to her rejection of his unvoiced love for her. Other eyes would have seen her running from the flagship seconds before the expedition's scheduled departure; and when he told them that she had decided to remain behind because of her love for a caveman, they would believe him.

With sinking heart she watched the long sleek lines of the seven ships rise steeply toward the blue and fade from sight. Never was she to see her world again, never to know the luxury and comforts of life as the ruler of half a planet.

Slowly she turned away from the disappearing link to the only life she had ever known. Her eyes sought out and found the figure of Valar still motionless by the tree.

In that moment she knew that fate had made for her the only decision that was right and good, and with singing heart and arms outspread she ran toward the man she loved.

THE END

If you've enjoyed this book, you will not want to miss these terrific titles…

ARMCHAIR SCI-FI & HORROR DOUBLE NOVELS, $12.95 each

D-91 **THE TIME TRAP** by Henry Kuttner
THE LUNAR LICHEN by Hal Clement

D-92 **SARGASSO OF LOST STARSHIPS** by Poul Anderson
THE ICE QUEEN by Don Wilcox

D-93 **THE PRINCE OF SPACE** by Jack Williamson
POWER by Harl Vincent

D-94 **PLANET OF NO RETURN** by Howard Browne
THE ANNIHILATOR COMES by Ed Earl Repp

D-95 **THE SINISTER INVASION** by Edmond Hamilton
OPERATION TERROR by Murray Leinster

D-96 **TRANSIENT** by Ward Moore
THE WORLD-MOVER by George O. Smith

D-97 **FORTY DAYS HAS SEPTEMBER** by Milton Lesser
THE DEVIL'S PLANET by David Wright O'Brien

D-98 **THE CYBERENE** by Rog Phillips
BADGE OF INFAMY by Lester del Rey

D-99 **THE JUSTICE OF MARTIN BRAND** by Raymond A. Palmer
BRING BACK MY BRAIN by Dwight V. Swain

D-100 **WIDE-OPEN PLANET** by L. Sprague de Camp
AND THEN THE TOWN TOOK OFF by Richard Wilson

ARMCHAIR SCIENCE FICTION CLASSICS, $12.95 each

C-31 **THE GOLDEN GUARDSMEN**
by S. J. Byrne

C-32 **ONE AGAINST THE MOON**
by Donald A. Wollheim

C-33 **HIDDEN CITY**
by Chester S. Geier

ARMCHAIR SCIENCE FICTION & HORROR GEMS SERIES, $12.95 each

G-9 **SCIENCE FICTION GEMS, Vol. Five**
Clifford D. Simak and others

G-10 **HORROR GEMS, Vol. Five**
E. Hoffman Price and others

GATEWAY TO A STRANGE, INNER WORLD

Commander Bob Allison was ready to take America's newest, flying military craft, The Annihilator II, *on its maiden voyage. It was indeed the most amazing flying vessel ever constructed, able to soar into outer space and cruise at speeds well over a thousand miles per hour. But a last-minute international disaster changed a maiden voyage into a rescue mission—a mission that would lead him and his crew to the top of the world in search of a lost Swedish research team. However, as the mighty craft drew near the North Pole, things took an odd, dangerous turn. Everything looked so strange. The sun didn't really look like the sun anymore. It was different, as was the sky above. Soon Allison and his crew found themselves captives in a fantastic world ruled by a savage lizard tribe and ravaged by hideous prehistoric beasts!*

CAST OF CHARACTERS

BOB ALLISON
He was the rugged commander of an amazing flying warship, and when ordered, was willing to fly it into any kind of danger.

JOAN HOLDON
Beautiful and brave—but it wasn't always easy being the fiancée of a man who might not come home from work alive.

LIEUTENANT-COMMANDER BRIGHT
Allison's First Officer. He was a bit of an eager beaver, but always good to have around when the going got tough.

RICHARD BRANDT
A condemned murderer whose broodings had created within him an insane hatred for all mankind.

HOKAR
Although he was a tribal chief, he was essentially nothing more than a big, vicious brute—with the head of a triceratops!

COMMANDER BARTLEY
Orders were orders to this seasoned executive officer, even if he did want to wring the necks of those issuing them!

SERGEANT RINGER
Although he was wounded, he later managed to be in just the right place at just the right time.

THE
ANNIHILATOR
COMES

By
ED EARL REPP

ARMCHAIR FICTION
PO Box 4369, Medford, Oregon   97501-0168

*For more information about Armchair Books and products, visit our
website at…*

www.armchairfiction.com

Or email us at…

armchairfiction@yahoo.com

CHAPTER ONE
The Promotion

IT did not take Lieutenant Robert Allison long to recover from the injuries he had received during the fateful maiden flight of the United States airship *Annihilator* when it was caught in the grip of a deadly Rocky Mountain updraft, and whisked upward so that it resisted the gravitational pull of the Earth.

Perhaps the most effective curative that had brought him around to normal after some weeks of convalescence in the base hospital at Rockwell Field, San Diego, was the almost constant presence of Joan Holdon. With her father, she had moved to San Diego from Denver, and taken up residence in the Lindbergh Aero-Hotel, just to be near him.

For many hours Allison had hovered between life and death after the *Annihilator* was rescued from the air-streams beyond gravity by the genius of Professor Stilsen. For hours each day Joan had sat at his bedside and watched the man of her choice emerge from oblivion and gradually regain the bloom of health. Then had come a day when attending physicians pronounced him completely recovered. His crushed ribs had knitted together and he had fought off the terrible effects of his tragic experiences.

Now, with Joan at his side, he walked through the hospital ward containing some of the *Annihilator's* convalescing crew and bade them goodbye. At the end of the hall a white-capped nurse was waiting for him, smiling.

"Well, Lieutenant, we're glad to see you in health again," she said. "You've been such a good patient that we'll all miss you. How do you feel, sir?"

She tapped her hand with a red, white and blue envelope and regarded him with a trained eye.

"Fine, Miss Hale," he replied, enthusiastically. "Couldn't be better. In fact I feel a hundred per cent better now than I did before the accident. Thanks to everyone here. But I'm mighty glad to be loose again..."

"I don't doubt it, Lieutenant," the nurse smiled. "Hospitals are one thing and freedom is another. It's hard to keep you flyers penned up for long. Here's a telegram that just arrived for you, sir."

She handed him the colored envelope and he tore it open excitedly. He knew it was from the government. Its color told him that and more. It had come from the Aviation Division, Department of War. He read it quickly and handed it to Joan, his brows clouding.

Lieutenant Robert Allison,
Base Hospital, Rockwell Field,
San Diego, California.

The War Department has this day commissioned you to command the Annihilator II stop Ship will be ready for flight ten days from date stop Report to Chief Commander Bartley at Kitty Hawk within ten days of your discharge from hospital for further orders stop Congratulations and regards

Secretary Aviation Division
War Department, U.S.A."

"Why, Bob!" Joan cried gleefully. "You've been promoted! That's wonderful! Just think of commanding another ship like the *Annihilator*..."

"But I hadn't expected the commission nor an order to report for duty so soon, Joan," he said, frowning. "I was hoping for an extended furlough until our plans materialized, at least. I don't like the idea, dear. It means that we'll have to postpone..."

"Oh, come on, Bob!" she said. "Our plans can wait until after you've reported. Perhaps we'll have the wedding ceremony at Kitty Hawk instead of here."

"I know, Joan," he insisted, "but what's a wedding without a honeymoon?"

She pulled at his sleeve mischievously and smiled into his face despite a tear that formed in her own eyes causing them to glisten like minute diamonds.

"The United States Government waits for no man, Robert," she said. "The wheels of war and conquest move despite the joys and sorrows of those concerned. You'll have to move with them. I'll be content to wait. We'll still have our future to look forward to, beloved. Delay will make our marriage sweeter..."

"I guess you're right, Joan," he said, resignedly. "We'll have to wait unless this order is just a preliminary one. I hope it is, and that I can return at once following my formal installation in command. I'm so stunned over it all that I can't think clearly!"

"It's wonderful!" Joan repeated. "Just think, they'll be saluting you as Commander Allison now..."

She stepped off a few paces and stood at attention. She brought her right hand upward in a stiff salute.

"I salute the commander of the great *Annihilator II,*" she said, impulsively. "And I pray that she will have better luck than her unfortunate sister who now lies buried in the…"

"Scrap yard!" he cut in, smiling and pulling her to him. "But let's forget about ships and scrap yards, Joan, and enjoy my few days of liberty together. You never can tell what the future holds for a flyer! Who knows, they might send the *Annihilator* around the world or on some other wild goose chase, the reason for which nobody, not even the War Department, knows!"

"Well, if they do, Robert," Joan said as they walked out of the hospital building, "you stay away from those Rocky Mountain up-drafts! I don't want you to get beyond gravity again. Perhaps you wouldn't come out quite so fortunately as you did this time…"

Holdon Gives Advice

COMMANDER ALLISON, his blue eyes flashing with happiness, followed Joan into her trim little aero-speedster with its transparent hummer wings, and sat down beside her. She tested the controls, stepped on the starter and shot the craft upward in a perpendicular ascent, its helicopters droning like miniature windmills. It hovered in mid-air for a moment while she turned on the pulling duals. Singing screws carried the craft as swiftly and gracefully as a humming-bird toward San Diego, which lay across the bay.

She looked downward upon Rockwell Field. It lay serene and calm with its brood of government planes. A few short weeks before, it had been the scene of much activity and apprehension, with the partially destroyed hulk of the *Annihilator* hanging above it in the grip of Professor

Stilsen's magnetic drums, which had coaxed her out of the distant heavens with her cargo of dying men. Joan shuddered, recalling certain scenes in which the man by her side had figured. She pictured them carrying his still, bloody form from the wreckage. There had been others, too, many others, who had not survived the ordeal and now lay under white crosses on the summit of Point Loma. A tear coursed down her cheek and she sought Bob's hand with trembling fingers.

"God has been good, Robert," she said. "Good to both of us. He saved your life for me."

He stared at her blankly for an instant and then nodded, glancing downward.

"I can imagine how you felt, Joan, when they carried me out of the wreck," he said. "It's odd that I should survive, hurt as I was, while others went west. Oh, well, it's all in the game of life. One fellow gets off while the other stands the gaff."

She squeezed his arm affectionately and concentrated on the controls. Straight ahead loomed the Lindbergh Aero-Hotel, rising into the heavens like a great, towering obelisk. Above it swarmed hundreds of craft, darting hither and yon like so many flies whose wings scintillated under the glare of a warm sun.

Joan cut her forward motors and whirled the helicopters for a vertical descent onto the flat top of the skyscraper. The little aero-speedster hovered and then dropped slowly. They hurried to the Holdon suite on a lower floor.

In the Holdon rooms, Joan's father nursed and cursed a cold in the head. When Joan and Bob arrived there, his valet was placing a bowl of mustard-water under his feet. Mr. Holdon was wrapped in a blanket and swearing softly under his breath.

"This darn cold!" he growled. "I'm the damndest—*ahhh-chew-w-w!* Unluckiest critter in forty-eight states. Who the devil said you can't catch a cold in San Diego? Ouch!" Mr. Holdon looked daggers at his valet.. "Get away from here and quit grinning. The water's too darn hot!"

"I'm sorry, sir," said the valet. "You asked for it hot, sir."

"I don't care what I asked for you damned idiot!" he snorted. "C-c-cool...*ahhh-chew!*...it off for me! Of all the blankety-blank..."

"Why, daddy..." Joan said remonstratingly. She and Bob had been standing just inside the door regarding the afflicted man as he sat in front of an open fireplace. "Aren't you ashamed to use such language!"

He looked up, his nose the color of a sun-reddened plum, his eyes as watery as his lips were colorless. Ex-Congressman Holdon always was subject to colds in the head and he was suffering one now in the act of becoming acclimated to San Diego's semi-tropical warmth—a decided change from the chill of the Rocky Mountain region whence he came.

"No I'm not ashamed," he grumbled. "This old damn cold is driving me crazy. The blankety-blank...oh, hell! What's the use..."

"Well you might have a little respect for me, daddy," said Joan. "And besides, I don't want Bob Allison to learn such talk."

"Good Lord, Joan," he gasped, "don't tell me you're going to make a ninny out of Bob Allison!"

"I'm not going to do that, daddy," she said, "but I'm not going to let you teach him your whole vocabulary, either. I brought him home with me and he's got some big news to tell you while I dress for dinner..."

Commander Bob Allison walked from his obscurity into the room, and Mr. Holdon rose to greet him.

"Bob…" he said, nodding to the valet to remove the bowl of mustard-water. "How do you feel, my boy?"

"Exceptional, Mr. Holdon." Bob nodded, taking the elder man's proffered hand. "Feel great! Sorry to see you in such bad shape."

"Me? Humph! I get a cold in the head every day before breakfast!" Holdon growled. "I'll be all right in a day or two. I'm mighty glad to see you, Robert. You know your father and I have been friends since we went to school and I sure have been worried about you!"

"Oh, I'm all right now, Mr. Holdon," said Bob. "I wired dad at Washington, telling him I've been turned loose and commissioned to command the sister ship of the *Annihilator.*"

"Command what?"

"Just as I was leaving the hospital I received an official telegram stating that the War Department has promoted me to commanding rank. I'm to command the *Annihilator II,* Mr. Holdon…"

"So that's the big news Joan hinted at, eh?"

"That's it, sir, but I wish they'd have waited until after Joan and I had had time to…"

"Get married, eh, Bobby?" Holdon interjected.

"Well, we sort of planned that, sir." Bob stammered, his face reddening. Joan's father was searching his eyes with a penetrating look. He straightened abruptly and projected his palm again.

"That's damn fine, Bob," he said. "So you've tamed that little wildcat, eh?"

"Tamed her?" Bob said. "No, it's the other way around, sir. She tamed me from the first."

Mr. Holdon laughed and sneezed and swore. He leaned closer to the son of his old friend, Senator Allison, and whispered guardedly.

"Well, here's a little advice, Bob," he said, winking. "Don't let her tame you too far, or she'll run over you like she has done to me. I've been a victim to her every whim, Robert. Make her eat out of your hand. You can do it…"

* * *

Time passed swiftly, perhaps too swiftly, for Commander Bob Allison and Joan Holdon. They spent five delightful days taking in the sights offered by beautiful San Diego, the great metropolis of the southwest. And many leisure hours were spent under the spreading boughs of the Spanish willows in Balboa Park.

Meanwhile Bob's strength rapidly returned. Each day he took his exercises, and Joan, with a sudden desire for the strenuous motions, joined him. Together they went through the routines in the modern gymnasium in the Lindbergh Aero-Hotel. Delightful hours spent at Mission Beach and at Coronado caused Bob's pallor to flee and a deep tan to take its place.

Then the day arrived for the flight from San Diego to Kitty Hawk across the continent, in Joan's little hummer plane. They took off on a bright morning and by midday were winging through Middle Western skies in well-established air lanes. Overhead raced the giant leviathans of aerial commerce. Great freighters laden with cargo, luxurious liners filled with passengers, scudded in all directions through the air.

It was the year 1980 and aviation had grown to far greater proportions than had been predicted in the earlier days of flying. Years before, railroading had been abandoned as slow and unprofitable, and the transportation companies had hurled themselves whole-heartedly into the field of aerial transportation. The world demanded speed and got it.

Bob watched a huge leviathan of the upper reaches scudding westward at a terrific clip. It looked like some gigantic kite racing through the heavens, unleashed, before a driving gale. The muffled roar of its giant screws reached their ears like the throb of thunder as it passed high overhead. It was one of the new liners recently put into the air by the Globe Circumvation Company, and was headed from the Atlantic coast to the Orient without a single stop. Quickly it vanished and those in Joan's plane turned to other interesting sights that marked their journey across the country.

CHAPTER TWO
A Dangerous Mission

CHIEF COMMANDER BARTLEY, stormy old petrel of the Kitty Hawk Division, American Air Forces, looked up from a pile of papers that lay upon the desk in his private sanctum at the "catbird air yards," and scowled. Around him sat a group of hard-faced young men, making up the commanding personnel of the *Annihilator II*. He waved a tri-colored paper over his head, glared at Commander Allison and swore under his breath at the others.

"Look at this, gentlemen!" he snapped loudly. "Look at this! Here's an order from Washington detailing the *Annihilator* to the North Pole to investigate the disappearance of a bunch of Swedes who went there looking for a place to plant their flag! For the life of me, gentlemen, I can't understand some of the crazy orders that come from those nincompoops behind roll-top desks in Washington. Now they order me to send the *Annihilator* to the pole when they know full well that she has not undergone her final tests. The bureaucratic idiots! It is my honest opinion that some of those men over us ought to be holding down muckers' jobs instead of responsible positions where they can sling men's lives around like so much ballast.

"Look at the original *Annihilator!* That's the result of Washington's orders. Rankin would not have taken the ship through the up-draft region had he not been instructed to do so through me by those nincompoops at the Capitol! Now I've got to send you boys out to look for a needle in the haystack just because the Swedish Government has asked us to search for its crazy explorers. It's hell, gentlemen..."

While Chief Commander Bartley glowered and hovered perilously close to the brink of insubordination, Commander Allison, looking as clean-cut and trim in his new uniform as a tailor's model, bit his lip abstractedly. Like all of the officers of the air forces, he understood the seeming inefficiency of some of the internal bureaus through which they were subject to many inconsiderate orders. But Commander Bob Allison was not thinking of bureaucratic nincompoops. He was thinking of those poor devils lost in the desolate wastes of the vast, worthless regions under the northern lights, and of Joan.

He had not expected to be sent with the *Annihilator* to such an out of the way place, with the date of his wedding drawing so near. What would Joan think about it? He wondered if he ought to resign his command and go to her, letting someone else worry about polar blasts, ice fields and arctic blizzards. He might be gone for months...might never return. Men have been lost forever in the arctic, even as the Swedes probably were now. Few ships, air or water, had been built to stand the strain.

But Bob Allison was not the kind of a man to quit in the face of peril. Deep within him, he felt an urge of adventure, the old flame that had drawn him into aviation from his early youth. He decided that Joan would have to wait until he returned. But the thought irked him and finally he cast it out of his mind, burying it in thoughts of personal duty to mankind. The lost creatures were men, flesh and blood like himself, and were therefore deserving of the respect of their fellows.

"Well, Commander," he said rising stiffly to attention, "I await your orders, sir. We shall start at your command, sir!"

Chief Commander Bartley, scowling into the papers on his desk, lifted his eyes and surveyed his subordinate, frowning; then pounded his fist on the arm of his chair.

"I've a damned good notion to wire those idiots in Washington to go plumb to hell, commander," he growled blackly. "But it would do no good. You'd have to go anyhow or...resign, sirrah."

"I had no thoughts of resigning, sir," Bob lied glibly. "In fact I'd welcome the chance to put the *Annihilator* through such a rigid test..."

"You would, eh?" the old man snorted, calming. "You would, sirrah?"

"Yes sir!" Bob saluted stiffly.

"Then by heavens you can go right ahead and do it!" the Chief Commander snapped, his eyes flashing with a trace of admiration for this newly installed officer. "But if you never get as far as the North Pole or even the Arctic Circle, don't tell me about it. Thank our Lord I'm not responsible for you, gentlemen. Good luck and good day, sirrahs!"

For several days the world's presses and televisions had told the world a graphic tale of tragedy at the northern extremities of the earth. Twenty Swedish explorers had gone to the north Polar Regions a year before to hunt for a new and undiscovered land under the aurora.

'They had set out from Skjangli near the northwestern frontier of Norway, expecting to return in the spring of the next year. The Swedish government had graciously turned over to them one of its finest scientifically equipped airliners, and they had set out to establish an operation base on Markham Island, the northernmost outpost of Greenland on the fringe of the Lincoln Sea. From there they were to scour the Polar Regions in one of the most extensive explorations in the history of arctic conquest.

One day in the spring Sweden had received word that its scientists had ended their research and that the liner was heading back toward Skjangli with very important information and new land for the nation that had made exploration possible. Radio-television, mounted in the R-T the room of the liner, informed the world that a very startling discovery had been made. But details were lacking, probably because the scientists withheld them until such times as the Swedish government decided to give out the news.

The Start!

THAT was all the world had ever heard from them. Then a frantic appeal had been sent out by Sweden asking the United States to help them rescue their scientists. Whether they had been grounded by a storm, nobody could tell, but that was generally conceded by American polar explorers to be the case. All agreed that their liner had crashed with tragic results, destroying lives and possibility of further communications.

It was a well-known fact that their provisions were perilously close to being exhausted. Two men, left at Markham Island, informed the world through a low wave radio-television broadcasting set, that their fellows would starve in less than thirty days unless help came to them. Just where the liner might be, the two men could not say, other than that the leader of the expedition had informed them that they were camped, before taking off to return home, at what they claimed was the *real geographic North Pole,* a spot which no known human being had ever located previously.

That bit of news caused many scientists to shake their heads incredulously, for during the years between 1935 and 1980, men had gone to the north and south polar regions and returned with what they declared were complete maps. How, then, at this late date, could the Swedish scientists discover some new land that did not exist on the allegedly accurate maps? Perhaps certain floes had melted; and it was quite unlikely, they believed, that a new land was revealed. At any rate, the men were lost and the *Annihilator* had been hurled into what Chief-Commander Bartley termed a mad search.

In consequence, Kitty Hawk suddenly became the scene of much activity. Men scurried hither and yon performing the duties incident to the taking off of the *Annihilator II* to search the arctic regions for twenty lost explorers. Elevators droned under the weight of provisions as foodstuffs and supplies were shot into its huge belly to be stored away for the officers, crews and additional men, should they locate the missing scientists.

Great stores of fuel, in the form of crusite powder for the ship's rocket driving exhausts, were placed in protected bunkers on the fuel decks. A thousand and one details had to be looked after in preparation for the first real flight of the sister ship of the destroyed *Annihilator I* in which Commander Bob Allison and hundreds of others had come so close to losing their lives.

Commander Allison, with a staff of alert, stiff-backed officers, attended to everything, supervising the loading of the supplies, arranging crews and whatnot necessary for a polar flight. As an additional precaution against unforeseen polar dangers, the young commander invited several American scientists and explorers to accompany them. His request for scientific help was immediately granted when he asked Chief-Commander Bartley to make his desires known in Washington.

Kitty Hawk was in fever heat. Every minute of time was needed. When the ship was ready, newspapermen with cameras and television-news operators were on hand to pay glowing tribute to the *Annihilator II* and its commanding officers. Commander Bob Allison received his share of the publicity, though he cared little for it. He was, to begin with, a great hero who had fought to the last to keep the *Annihilator I* from being pulled into the distant skies beyond the influence of gravity while in the grip of the deadly up draft near Denver. All this was recalled by newspapermen. With it went the news that he had been given the rank of commander and would have full charge of the *Annihilator II*.

Then Allison stood on the enclosed bridge just over the control cabin in the *Annihilator's* geometrically shaped nose and gave orders for takeoff. Far below he caught a glimpse of Joan and her father standing on the fringe of an excited crowd. Her face was hidden behind a handkerchief, but her father was appraising the ship intently.

Allison felt a pang of remorse when he looked down upon his betrothed. She had not objected to his going to the North Pole or anywhere. Instead, she had urged him to do his duty, vowing to wait for him until the sun sank forever. But he wondered, as the *Annihilator* rose vertically, if he would be as fortunate in returning to her this time as he had been from the disastrous flight of the craft's sister-ship.

Northward Bound

OUTWARDLY, there was little difference in the appearance of the *Annihilator II* and that of her junked sister. But internally, the new craft had incorporated many radical changes and improvements including up-to-the-minute devices in case of a repetition of the former craft's destruction. Science had learned many things in the meantime.

Where the destroyed craft had been built to nullify gravity only to a certain degree, the *Annihilator II* was capable of almost entirely overcoming the earth's gravitational influence. Had this been within the power of the former ship, the disaster might not have occurred, for she could have gone above the air-streams that had held her, and returned to earth at will. As it was, she could repel gravity only up to a certain altitude, then hover under its influence, unable to rise further.

But when government scientists and engineers had finished the *Annihilator II,* they pronounced her capable of overcoming gravity to the extent that interplanetary travel was not at all beyond the realms of possibility. Through the installation of more powerful dynamos that supplied the electro-magnetic power for her great, cobalt-steel hull, she could rise to almost unlimited heights, falling away from the globe without interference from its gravitational forces.

As a precaution against unforeseen obstacles in the generation of electro-magnetic power for gravity nullification, the *Annihilator II,* like her sister, contained a set of safety airfoils that extended outward from the hull. In the event that the forces within her that nullified gravity should suddenly or unexpectedly fail to operate, throwing the ship under the influence of the earth's pull, these airfoils could be utilized for gliding. But there was little fear of a disaster of this order, for the ship contained dual dynamos with one unit held always in reserve.

In the field of propulsion, the great ship departed abruptly from all others outside of her class. She contained a powerful rocket drive system, using crusite powder as fuel for the internal combustion chambers. This powder was fired in relays, creating a tremendous force that hurled the ship through the air as the spent gases were vented through a series of exhausts.

As for the remainder of the *Annihilator II,* she was precisely the same in general construction as her unfortunate sister ship. At the geometrical nose was the control cabin. Above this, surrounded by observation exposures of thick quartz, was the bridge from which the commanding officers sent their orders by radio-television to even the remotest corners of the craft. Now, as Commander Robert Allison stood on the bridge with a group of subordinates around him and watched the rapidly diminishing forms of the spectators, the *Annihilator II* shot swiftly skyward. Already the drive exhausts were hissing with potent, thrusting energy, and, as she rose higher, dousing her hull in a bank of mists, she began to move northward.

At 60,000 feet, she was scarcely visible to those who stood upon the ground and watched her depart, held in breathless awe by the glorious sight. She emerged from the mists and the sun struck her broadside as the drive exhausts vomited long jets of blazing fire. Those on the ground saw her hull glisten in the sun. She hissed across the heavens like a meteor, gaining altitude as she went.

Commander Bob Allison stood at the radio-television broadcast and receiving set on the bridge of the *Annihilator* and spoke calmly into the speaking piece. His voice and image were carried at once to the control room.

"Take her up to ninety thousand, Lieutenant..." he ordered. "Set your course due north for the geographic pole; then open her up."

Lieutenant Berger, sitting calmly at the main control, peered into the calm features of Commander Allison in the oval television screen resting among the instruments on the board in front of him.

"Yes, sir," he nodded, smiling grimly, his features hardset.

He moved slowly a small wheel that lay in the center of the control and regarded his instruments. The altimeter needle was turning swiftly to the right. He checked its readings mentally and then snapped the wheel into the 90,000 notch. The altimeter needle stopped at that altitude, quivering like an arrow imbedded in a wall. He cast a quick glance at a brother officer sitting at the reserve controls at his right and grinned.

"The old man seems to have lost some of his nerve since the crack-up of the old *Annihilator,* Cameron," he said. "He doesn't seem to be his old reckless self. If the Bob Allison I used to know was in command of this ship, he'd send her to Mars to he sure of altitude!"

Lieutenant Cameron nodded.

"Maybe he wants to be careful this time," he said, studying his instruments. "I don't blame him if he's a little more safety-minded."

"Neither do I, Lieutenant," said Berger, increasing the acceleration, "but he ought to take her up out of the rest of this atmospheric resistance."

"He knows what he's doing," said Cameron. "You ought to be glad that he's lost some of his old-time recklessness. I am, old sox! No need to take unnecessary chances."

"But I fear he's lost some his nerve," Berger insisted. "We're losing time by flying in this resistance. He ought to take her up another 30 miles at least. I'd like to get back home again. I've no stomach for this North Pole stuff..."

A Sudden Danger

BUT Commander Allison had not lost his nerve. Nor was he being unduly cautious. His order to fly the *Annihilator* at the 90,000-foot altitude was quite justifiable in view of his desire to put her to a resistance test before going into the rarefied regions of space where friction diminishes so rapidly. He stood before the instrument panel on the bridge and studied the maze of dials, meters and levels that confronted him. His trained eyes read them rapidly and he turned to his next ranking officer.

"She cuts the air like an arrow, Bright," he said, growing more pleased with the performance of the *Annihilator* with each passing moment. "I think she's going to prove to be a better ship than the old *Annihilator.*"

"She's doing fine, Commander," Lieutenant-Commander Bright nodded. "I'm anxious to see what she can turn up in the face of resistance."

"She's doing five hundred now, but she ought to increase that by half against friction," said Bob. "If she's got more velocity than the old ship, she ought to kick out about a thousand miles per hour."

"Dr. Shelton, head of the science department back at the cat-bird yards, said he thought she'd do better," said

Bright, cocking an eye at his superior. "He gave her velocity in the rarefied regions as unlimited."

Bob nodded and gave an order into the speaking tubes of the ship's communication apparatus. Almost at once they felt the *Annihilator* lurch ahead under added force, and her speed increased swiftly until the dials indicated that she was clipping off 900 miles per hour flat. The velocity indicator paused there as the *Annihilator* raced northward, passed over the United States Capitol, left it behind like a white mound, and settled down to her great race to the pole.

In gradual ascents, she was lifted high above the commercial air lanes and gradually the details of the land below became only a blur. Then a blanket of mist shut out the earth for a time as completely as though it did not exist.

Commander Bob Allison remained at the instrument panel. Few orders were necessary now. Every man within the *Annihilator* knew his business and attended to it with regulation precision. Occasionally Allison studied the jets of pale blue flame that shot from the craft's exhausts, hissing ominously like some prehistoric carnivorous reptile of the air. Then the mist cleared and he found himself staring down upon the towering obelisks of New York City. They looked like toothpicks stuck within a web of hair. He had given an order for the ship to swing a trifle east of its course to pass over Gotham. No time was lost; he wanted to give its seething millions the thrill of seeing the craft blazing through the upper reaches like a glistening needle. But New York passed almost suddenly out of sight and the *Annihilator's* nose was swung due north again.

As the Great Lakes stood under his feet like little puddles of water surrounded by the snow-clad cities and open areas around them, Bob noticed a group of peculiar white lights, visible even in the light of midday, a few points off the port stream-lines. They seemed like tiny pinpoints but were growing in size gradually and he looked quickly at the meteorometer. The needle was jerking spasmodically to port, and he gasped.

The growing lights were fireballs and he calculated that, with the velocity of both the *Annihilator* and the celestial missiles, they would come into each other's right-of-way within two minutes. Instantly he grabbed the speaking tube and yelled into it tensely.

"Pull her down to a hundred thousand feet, Lieutenant!" he snapped. "Fire-balls off the port!"

With a feeling of nausea in his vitals, he felt the *Annihilator* drop like an express elevator. A rapidly approaching roar told him that the blazing missiles were coursing overhead to smash into the Earth somewhere or continue on around it. He seemed to feel the electro-magnetic energy surging through the *Annihilator's* cobalt-steel hull, and the falling sensation ceased slowly. She had dropped out of the path of the missiles and was coursing northward again in the heavier atmospheres.

Commander Allison might have turned all the details of direction over to his staff and taken himself to the comfort of his own well-appointed cabin, but he preferred to remain on the bridge. He did not believe himself any more capable of handling the flight than any of the others of his staff, yet he derived certain pleasure from standing on the bridge of his very own command to see that every detail was carried out to the perfection that made the United States Air Forces supreme the world over. Being the young man that he was, there were particular thrills in the flight that held him tensely at the instrument board, occasionally watching the snow-clad world below him pass by.

Finally he issued the order for the craft to rise again to the fifty-mile altitude. She went up rapidly as the gravity repellent shot through the hull. He watched the scenes below merge into a jumbled nothing. Clouds and mists, storms of snow and rain surged below, finally hiding the surface entirely.

CHAPTER THREE
The Deserted Men

THE Hudson Bay, according to the ship's instruments, lay under the *Annihilator*. Bob checked his charts and with a pencil marked the course. In another hour the *Annihilator*, under her present velocity of 1500 miles per hour, would be across Canada and the Northwest Territories. Then she would be entering the desolate wastes of the far north. From then on a close watch must be maintained for traces of the lost explorers.

Thin coatings of frost had already begun to mar the quartz in the observation panels. Inside the *Annihilator* it was as warm as toast, the heat coming from a ventilation system which carried warmth from the hot combustion chambers. The officers had long since removed their "monkey suits" with fur-lined interiors, and were comfortable enough in the trim jackets, boots and breeches of their respective ranks.

Commander Bob felt a sudden impulse to communicate with the two men the Swedish explorers had left behind at their base on Markham Island. He picked up the speaking piece of the ship's communication instruments and got in touch with the radio-television operator, ordering him to communicate at once with the two men to learn if any word had come from the lost scientists.

The operator called the commander presently and Bob had a glimpse of a haggard face in the bridge television screen. The fellow wore a long beard that almost completely hid his worn features. He was blowing blasts of steam from his lips as he spoke. He looked like some shaggy brute, savage and ready to snap.

"Markham Island?" Bob inquired, staring at the man's features. The fellow answered in fairly good English.

"Yes, sir!" he said. "Markham Island operation headquarters, Swedish Polar Expedition."

"Any word from the lost men?" Bob asked. Lieutenant-Commander Bright looked over his shoulder into the screen.

"I've picked up some faulty messages that I could not understand, Commander," the shaggy one said, breathing excitedly. "I don't know where they come from, but my direction indicator pointed toward the polar cap. I thought I caught my name mentioned, but it might have come from one of the rescue ships already on the field."

"Oh, then others have beat us, eh?"

"Our government has had several planes and ships in the vicinity for weeks, sir," he said. "The *Annihilator* is the first alien craft to appear. Have you got any medicine aboard, sir?"

"Yes, why?" asked Bob.

"My partner is down flat with pneumonia and I can do nothing for him," the man groaned. "I'm all alone and not feeling any too well myself."

"We'll drop a serum to you on our way over," Bob said.

"That's fine, sir," the man at the outpost smiled. "But can't you pick us up instead?"

"I think it best for you to remain where you are," Bob asserted. "Your men might communicate with you. I can't spare a relief. You'll be all right."

"But I'll go insane staying here alone. My partner is raving…"

"I might pick him up, but you'll have to stay," Bob insisted. "We'll take you on later...in a couple of days if not before. But say, what the devil's wrong with your face? What are those red marks under your eyes?"

The man gasped and ran a nervous hand over his exposed cheekbones.

"Red marks?" he said, weirdly. "Good lord...have I got it, too?"

"Got what?" Bob snapped.

Lieutenant-Commander Bright nudged Bob and whispered. "The man's got small-pox, Commander," he said. "Bet his partner is down with it..."

Then the man spoke again.

"I might as well tell you, sir," he said, "that my partner is down with small-pox. He must've got it from a band of Esquimaux that passed by here a week ago. We bought some walrus blubber from them."

"Then I'm mighty sorry, old timer," Bob said softly, "that we can't pick up either one of you. But we'll drop medicines and serums for you. Hard luck... It's against orders to take on anything like that. Stand by to pick up the delivery..."

Commander Allison swung from the screen and picked up an intercommunication tube. He pressed a button beside the oval screen and waited for the hospital attendant to answer. The medico's face appeared almost at once.

"Prepare a chest of small-pox serums to be dropped overboard at once, doctor," Bob ordered crisply. "Have it delivered immediately to the bridge."

The *Annihilator* turned her nose slightly north by northeast across the arctic archipelago known as the Parry Islands, and headed for Markham Island, lying off the northernmost extremities of Greenland. She opened her exhausts and pressed against a head-on gale that was sweeping down upon her in a terrific blast. For a half-hour she shot across the bleak wastes scarcely more than 40,000 feet up; then she dropped down to 20,000.

The Arctic Ocean was frozen over and covered with snow. There was not a sight of land to be had from any side; the whole thing looked like a great field of ice, packed and caked into a rugged, awe-inspiring mass. Eagle-eyed observers, standing on the warm bridge, studied the scene under and before the *Annihilator's* nose through powerful telescopes for a glimpse of a snow-clad shack.

Allison Decides

IT was a difficult undertaking, even through telescopes, to find a tiny ice-covered hut nestling snugly on a bleak, white world. And the added interference of a howling blizzard served to increase the observers' apprehension and their growing doubts of locating the outpost, which contained two suffering remnants of a once seemingly indomitable scientific expedition. But finally it was spotted, mapped and logged. From a 1,000-foot altitude the shack looked like a tiny square of dirty white standing out in base relief from the general surface of the ice fields. Smoke from a chimney had showered the roof with a smudge, breaking the monotony of endless whiteness.

The *Annihilator* slowed its velocity, circled over the hut at a low elevation and whirled its sirens. Almost at once a fur-clad figure emerged from it, shielded his face from the blasts of snow and ice and cutting winds, and looked up. Then he waved his arms wildly—insanely.

Commander Allison watched him standing below, waist-deep in snow, and felt a pang of pity for him. The two men must have suffered untold agonies of privation here on this bleak, snow-swept island, and now one was down with smallpox; the other threatening to drop at any moment. He looked at the medicine chest lying on the floor of the bridge waiting for some hand to drop it through the life-saving chute which yawned under a beryllium hatch-covering. Undoubtedly both men would die even with medicines, before they might return. It was certain that the man standing in the blizzard would go down. Then without help they would both die of starvation if not from the ravages of the dread disease.

Bob's features suddenly became hard and his eyes flashed decisively. He shot an order into the tubes and turned to the warrant officer.

"Rogers," he snapped, "have the chief quartermaster send out a land party to bring in the two men! See that they are inoculated beforehand. Have the two men from the hut placed in solitary confinement and have Doctor Riorden attend to them."

"Yes, sir!" the man saluted, striding swiftly to the speaking tubes.

The *Annihilator* settled slowly toward the ice, one of her great airfoils sheltering the tiny hut that lay under it. There was a general scurry of activity in all quarters as men were detailed to bring in the afflicted men. From the bridge, Bob and his staff watched the man dancing joyously in the snow. He turned to Lieutenant-Commander Bright and swore.

"It's against orders, Bright," he said, "but I'll be damned if I'll leave those poor devils here to die. I can't see how they can spread the disease if measures are taken to prevent it..."

"Amen!" said Bright. "It would be a rotten crime to let 'em rot without help. It's a humanitarian act, sir, to take 'em aboard. But what about a relief? Are you leaving the radio station in the hut unattended?"

"No, I'm going to ask for two volunteers from our radio-television crew, and let them take care of the outpost until we fly over again," Bob said curtly. He turned to the warrant officer again.

"Rogers," he said, "have your R-T crew report to me at once…"

While Warrant Officer Rogers was relaying his orders, Bob watched the outpost attendant fighting madly through the snow to reach the *Annihilator*. He stumbled many times, got up weakly, and struggled onward. Then a squad of men from the *Annihilator* was seen plunging toward him. He collapsed in the snow just as they reached his side, and was placed upon a stretcher and carried out of sight. The remainder of the squad continued on to the hut and vanished within it. They emerged presently carrying a still form.

Commander Allison turned away to appraise a group of R-T men lined at attention on the bridge.

"Men," he said, "bringing those two scientists aboard has left the outpost unattended. It is important that it be kept open in case the lost men try to communicate with it by radio. I want two volunteers to relieve them until we determine whether or not the lost members of the expedition live. Who will remain behind?"

Instantly the entire group stepped forward. As one man, they all volunteered, despite the fact that none of them harbored a genuine desire to be left like ice particles on the vast, unknown, frozen wastes.

Commander Allison, knowing many of the operators personally, expected just such a move. He chose two. The men saluted with pleasure.

"That's fine, boys," he said, temporarily shunning the dignity of his rank and striding forward. "It won't be for long. Good luck to you both."

The men shook hands and were dismissed. At the companionway leading from the bridge down to the main promenade deck, one turned and waved. The youthful commander nodded and returned the salute.

As a precaution against the spreading of the disease, every man on board the *Annihilator* who had not been recently vaccinated was subjected to an inoculation of smallpox serum. Then the *Annihilator* rose a thousand feet and began a slow zigzagging course toward the geographic North Pole.

Was It a Dream?

THE blizzard increased in fury until the wind shrieked along the streamlined hull of the *Annihilator,* drowning the moaning hiss of her exhausts. Particles of ice smashed against the observation exposures and the going had to be slow to maintain a close lookout for traces of the lost explorers.

At times the craft was sent so low that her glistening, frost-coated bottom scarcely cleared the jagged ice that piled high in mountainous shapes. On the great ice field they eventually came upon a snowed-in Esquimaux town. The craft paused, shrieked its sirens, and went on after a reasonable delay. There were no men venturing outside in the little circle of igloo huts; there was nothing to indicate even that life existed in the ice-clad town. But those on board the *Annihilator* knew that the inhabitants were content to remain within their mound-shaped dwellings, protected against the terrible blasts that swept down upon them from the North. Had Americans been in camp, they would have exposed themselves at the first whining sound of the *Annihilator's* earsplitting sirens.

The great airship swept over the desolate wastes at a velocity of little more than fifty miles per hour now. Only one of her exhausts belched a throttled stream of flame. Below, the scenes remained unchanged. Vast fields of unbroken desolation lay on every hand, staring lifelessly at the leviathan of the air.

Gradually the blizzard subsided as the *Annihilator* cruised steadily northward in sweeping zigzags. Tense observers stood on the bridge and studied every mile as it passed by, but they saw nothing but occasional wolves— great, scraggy creatures that almost merged with the harmony of the north. One pack, hunger-crazed, raced over the ice under the ship for miles, like sharks following in the wake of a doomed vessel.

Crews were changed with clock-like regularity in the *Annihilator*, but Bob Allison remained on the bridge for a long time. Suddenly one of the men yelled jubilantly and pointed downward. Bob grabbed a glass and studied what appeared to be the wreck of an airplane partially covered with snow, the tip of an airfoil showing and a tail sticking up in the air at a sharp angle. He observed a thin wisp of smoke curling upward from the wreckage.

Instantly the *Annihilator* shut off her exhaust and hovered, finally settling on the ice beside the wrecked plane. All hands were turned to at once, and the plane was surrounded by a group of eager men. But to the intense chagrin and disappointment of the *Annihilator's* officers and crew, it was discovered that only one man out of the plane's crew of eight was living! They found him squatting, half-frozen, before a small fire fueled from the wreckage. The others lay dead around him, stark proof of the failure of one of the Swedish rescue planes that had set out to find their brothers.

The man's features were ghastly. Pieces of flesh hung down from beneath his eyes, cracked off by the killing frost and cold. His fingers and toes were black, dead things and had to be amputated in the *Annihilator's* surgical chamber. The dead men were buried in holes dug in the ice and covered with the motors of the plane as a precaution against the predatory creatures of the polar wilds.

Following the discovery of the unfortunate rescue party, Commander Allison sought the solace of his cabin, undressed, and retired. But he had no more than gotten well to sleep, it seemed to him, than he was awakened by Lieutenant-Commander Bright. The ship's barometers had fallen to zero, creating alarm and apprehension among the officers who were aware of what the drop in the recording of the storm instruments meant.

But what held Commander Allison's eyes riveted ahead was a vast body of water, open and free from ice. It was rolling gently like some great inland lake. He turned presently and studied his charts, suspecting that the *Annihilator's* speed had been increased during the night, taking her well away from the north Polar Regions. But he was amazed to learn that she was flying as slowly as before, and was over the geographic pole!

He looked again at the rolling body of water, rubbing his eyes. Had he suddenly been transferred in his dreams to some strange magical land? A great bird, with a wingspread of a dozen feet, flapped across his vision toward the distant horizon. Was it possible that such a bird could be flying serenely over the North Pole? But there it was, nevertheless, and those on board the *Annihilator* were stunned by its sudden, unexpected appearance.

CHAPTER FOUR
The Pole or the Tropics?

PROFESSOR MARBLE, head of the division of vertebrate mammals of the Johnsonian Institution, stood beside Commander Allison. On the other side of him was Dr. Ralston of the same institution, from which the government recruited its staff of scientists to accompany the *Annihilator.* They were studying the bird through powerful glasses. They saw it hover on the horizon for an instant and then dive suddenly out of sight!

"That was a species of bird that has long since been extinct, to our knowledge!" Professor Marble exclaimed. "It was a pterodactyl or I'm as crazy as a loon!"

"Pterodactyl is correct, professor," agreed Dr. Ralston. "Mighty strange, but correct. I can't believe it..."

"But what about this body of water, gentlemen?" Bob asked blankly. "My charts don't show any bodies of water this far north, and besides, they give our location at exactly the spot where the true geographic pole ought to be."

Professor Marble looked at the commander intently, and then blurted out:

"Are you sure you read your charts correctly, commander?" he asked.

Bob's face reddened under his tan, but he smiled easily.

"I've been reading charts too long, professor," he said quickly, "to make such an error..."

"There's no mistake, professor," said Lieutenant-Commander Bright. "We're over the true pole right enough, but there seems to be a fly in the ointment somewhere. I've been on the bridge for hours, and we've maintained our course straight for the pole."

"But this water and the bird, gentlemen," insisted the scientist, "are completely baffling. If we are at the true pole, then other explorers have erred, because we have no record of a body of water this far north; And it's warm water, too..."

"Reminds me of Marshall B. Gardner's theories of a temperate zone in the arctic," Dr. Ralston interjected, "but of course little credence has ever been placed in that. In his book he contended that the true pole had never been discovered."

"But that's not altering our situation, gentlemen," said Bob. "We're either at the North Pole or we're not. I confess that I'm mystified. The whole thing is a mystery beyond my powers of comprehension; the lake, the bird and what appears to be an overcast, semitropical country."

"Well, there must be some sort of land just beyond the horizon," said Professor Marble, "otherwise that bird would not have plunged straight down. The pterodactyl is a land bird, not an amphibian. I suggest that we cruise along over there and investigate. Perhaps our missing men discovered this mystery and went further to look into it and became lost somewhere beyond."

"That's a logical idea," said Dr. Ralston.

"We'll go over and have a look." Bob nodded, turning to Bright. "Change her course north by northwest."

A Strange World

As the *Annihilator* proceeded on her new course, those on the bridge were treated to a strange sight in the water below. From an altitude of several hundred feet, the water in the mysterious lake appeared as transparent as a great sheet of thick glass. They could see great schools of fish churning through the water on every hand. Frequently huge water mammals blew the surface and they caught sight of tremendous snouts and great, spread jaws. The water was fairly alive with organisms of one sort or another. Immense shoals of savage-looking fish swam, feeding, in the wake of retreating schools. Then they had a glimpse of a great sun that seemed to rise in front of the ship. It literally popped up and stood in the heavens a few degrees above the horizon.

Commander Allison ordered the *Annihilator* directly into the sun, for it lay in the course taken by the huge bird. Speeding in that direction at a velocity that was now little less than 200 miles per hour, the *Annihilator* went hissing over the great lake like some huge bird of prey. Gradually the water became more shallow as they could easily see from the altitude, and presently it lapped placidly on a shore that was lined with tropical vegetation. Had they been flying around some inland sea along the equator, they could have been in no more tropical territory than that which lay spread out before their eyes!

Great flocks of vari-colored birds scattered before the huge leviathan of mankind and took refuge in what appeared to be an impenetrable jungle. The sun still lay ahead, just above the horizon, casting warmth over a tropical land that lay beneath its beams. Was this ball of fire the central sun in the interior of the earth, as theorized, back in 1920, by that brilliant scientist Marshall B. Gardner, whose interesting book* had sought to prove that the poles

---

* "A Journey Into the Earth's Interior" or "Have the Poles Really Been Discovered?" published in 1920 by Marshall B. Gardner, its author.

had never really been discovered? Was this great ball of fire the flaming core of the earth or was it actually a central sun spraying an interior world with life-giving properties?

Professor Marble found himself speculating upon these thoughts as the *Annihilator* continued across the matted jungles that lay under her belly. It was very hard for him to concede that Gardner's theories concerning an interior world within our globe were correct. He recalled the famous book and reasoned that the theorist had offered a sound enough argument, yet it was hard to believe that within the confines of the icy north a tropical land could exist, teeming with a life that should have passed out of existence thousands of years ago.

Great birds with membranous wings and long, saw-toothed beaks took wing from the higher rocks in the jungle and flapped slowly away at the approach of the *Annihilator*. Marble finally decided, as the ship slowed down its velocity for an investigation into the mystery, that here was some great valley that the passing of centuries had in no way affected with a change of life. But how could such a valley exist at the North Pole? By the time the *Annihilator* grounded her gear on a flat, grassy meadow in the heart of the strange, teeming jungle, Professor Marble began to concede that there might be something after all in Gardner's theories. And before the search for the lost Swedish scientists had come to an end, he was destined to credit those theories whole-heartedly.

There has always been something of a mystery surrounding the discovery of the huge ice-encrusted masto-don by the Tongoose fisherman, Schumachoff, in the Arctic Circle. Professor Marble, like many another scientist, had marveled at that discovery of the mammoth held in a perfect state of preservation by a refrigeration of ice, and had wondered whence it had come. Now Marble and the others on board the *Annihilator* were seeing with their own eyes the very jungles that had undoubtedly reared that same mammal countless centuries before.

As the *Annihilator* shut off her exhausts and her officers prepared a scouting party, those on the bridge saw a herd of huge, towering mastodons thundering away from the meadow. There must have been fifty beasts in the great herd, their long, up-curling tusks standing out before their heads, shoving small trees aside as though they were match-sticks. The thunder of their pounding feet caused the earth to tremble as they stampeded away.*

But would the lost Swedish explorers be found in this strange world? It was only natural for Commander Allison and those under him to believe that they would be. Word received by the Markham Island base of the expedition had told that the scientists had been camped at what they said was the true North Pole. Perhaps they had encountered the mysterious open lake and followed it until they became lost in a strange, tropical domain. Bob had little doubt that they would be found somewhere in the teeming world and he was now prepared to search for them.

---

* It was Marshall Gardner who first offered an argument as to the source of the preserved mastodon. He had fought a bitter battle with orthodox science in an effort to prove that the mastodon had come from a tropical world inside of the earth. But strangely, little faith was placed in his theories. However, there was no denying them now! The interior of the earth was a world in itself, a warm tropical world which thundered with the teeming life that on the exterior had long been extinct. It had its own sun, the flaming mass which orthodox science claimed was merely the core of the earth; it had its own lakes, its own atmosphere. The *Annihilator* had unconsciously entered it through the northern entrance, an open polar cap 1400 miles across, and was now under an 800 mile thick earth crust upon which humanity subsisted.

Exciting Moments

HAD he been an older man and less imbued with the spirit of adventure, he might have placed a subordinate in charge of the scouting expedition and taken himself to the safety of his cabin. But Bob Allison had a desire to be in the thick of things, especially if adventure beckoned. And adventure called him strongly; he could not resist going at the head of the party into this strange land on whose every side strange beasts peered at the invaders.

Armed to the teeth with powerful rifles that shot explosive projectiles, they crossed the meadow in the direction taken by the herd of mammoths. Keen-eyed observers had spotted, in the valley beyond, what appeared to be the tail sections of a wrecked airship. There was no way of telling exactly what it was when the *Annihilator* flew over it because of the harmonious color-scheme of the jungle. And the wreckage had appeared smoke-blackened, leading Bob to believe that the Swedish ship had crashed and burned on the spot.

At the head of fifty armed members of his crew, and flanked by Professor Marble, Dr. Ralston and Lieutenant-Commander Bright, Bob led the party down into a ravine to the edge of a swamp. A huge dinosaur stood in the center of the pool, lapping lily pads as unconcernedly as a domestic cat drinking milk out of a saucer. The beast looked up calmly and scrutinized the party, then lumbered away, its great reptilian tail swaying from side to side.

"Good Lord, commander!" ejaculated Professor Marble, trembling with excitement. "That was an herbivorous dinosaur! Why, from all understanding of modern science, that beast should have been extinct for a million years! What do you think of it, Dr. Ralston?"

Dr. Ralston stood at the edge of the swamp and studied the huge dinosaur tracks, exactly like those preserved in the asphalt beds of Wyoming and Nebraska; then he shook his head blankly.

"Damned if I can think anything, Marble…" he said incredulously. "I can't believe my eyes. But undoubtedly the beast was an herbivorous dino."

Suddenly the air was rent with a scream of terrible agony. Every single member of the party automatically gripped his gun. The scream was inhuman, like the maniacal shriek of some primeval beast in the throes of death. Then there was a commotion on the other side of a medium-sized pool. A horrible-looking creature had emerged from the water and grasped a small animal of the primate class, and was chewing it savagely. It was a great, ferocious marine lizard thirty feet long, and it was retreating into the water again with its victim between its saw-edged teeth. Instinctively Bob raised his explosive-throwing pistol and let fly. The pistol cracked softly but the explosion of the missile inside the lizard sent a thunderous report reverberating through the jungles.

The lizard's head was torn from its body and the creature fell to the shallow water, thrashing madly, its great tail beating the water and throwing a warm spray over those who watched. Then its death struggles ceased and it lay still, half-submerged in the stagnant pool. The men went around to the other side and Professor Marble, after a brief study of the creature, declared that it bore complete resemblance to remains of such lizards taken from the chalk-beds of Kansas and Missouri.

Then pandemonium seemed to break loose! The explosion of Bob's missile had awakened the dismal jungles around them, and creatures went crashing through the matted entanglements on every side. The herd of mastodons thundered down the ravine, trumpeting in a terrifying manner. Towering dinosaurs, herbivorous and carnivorous, rose from the brush, stared at the strange creatures that had suddenly come among them, and raced away. And the pool boiled under the lashing of tremendous tails, snapping jaws and swimming water denizens, frightened by the sudden concussion.

Stupefied at the abrupt uproar and the many strange beasts around them, the party stood stock-still and stared, open-mouthed. Commander Allison, his pistol half-raised, was watching the approach of the mastodons. They came roaring down the valley toward them at a terrific speed. The ground seemed to tremble with the rise and fall of their thunderous feet. Horrifying blasts rent the silence as the herd crashed down upon the party with renewed speed.

Bob's pistol cracked again and again, and each time the crash of a giant body followed the roar of exploding missiles that mangled the beasts horribly. Then the whole party sprang into action. Rifles were lifted to strong shoulders and they belched death into the herd. But so mad was its rush that the remaining members came on like express trains, clearing the fallen beasts in wild leaps. Bob dropped a leading mammal; then his pistol snapped, empty. Rapidly the rifles cracked until half the herd lay dead or dying.

Seeing that the beasts were bent upon running them down, Bob ordered a retreat as the herd swung upon them. The party scattered immediately into the jungles to escape the enraged beasts. Bob, with his first officer Bright, sought the safety of a huge tree that swung spreading branches over the jungle level. Scarcely had they departed from the dead water-lizard than the remainder of the mastodon herd roared past and crashed away.

Commander Allison re-loaded his heavy pistol as he sat in a crotch of the tree and jammed it into his waist holster. Lieutenant-Commander Bright sat on a higher branch above and grinned, but his face was pale.

"Narrow escape, Commander," he said, trembling. "They'd have trampled the whole party in another minute!"

"I thought we could stop the stampede," said Bob, glancing below him. "But evidently there's no stopping those beasts when they get started. Quite an odd experience for a modern man, eh?"

"Odd?" queried Bright. "Odd, hell! Its stupefying, sir!"

Bob chuckled softly and looked at his subordinate quizzically.

"Not scared, are you, Bright?" he quizzed.

"Not exactly, sir," declared Bright, truthfully. "But I had a few funny sensations running through my innards when I saw that herd pounding down upon us. You could call it fright if you want to…"

"I suppose we all experienced sinking sensations, Bright," said Bob, peering into the branches above him. "Its no crime for a man to get rattled under conditions like these…"

On the jungle floor beneath him, Bob thought he detected a slight movement. Looking down, he saw a huge sabre tooth tiger approaching stealthily. Instinctively he drew his pistol and waited. Bright glanced down, yelled, and swung down from his perch away from the approaching menace. Bob drew a bead on the carnivore and fired. The head vanished with a crimson explosion and the giant tree shook madly from the death-throes of the dying monstrosity. Its massive carcass lurched and collided with the tree in a final death-thrust. It caught Bob by surprise and sent him spinning into the lower branches, clutching frantically. His pistol dropped to the ground as he grasped at the twisted boughs. There he hung, gasping for breath; then let himself safely to the ground.

Lieutenant-Commander Bright was waiting for him. He had recovered the pistol and was re-loading the empty chamber.

"Hurt, sir?" he asked, handing over Bob's gun.

"Knocked the breath out of me, Bright," he said, still gasping. "Cripes, what a beast... Must be thirty feet long!"

"You should have dropped out of the tree when I did, Commander," said Bright. "We had plenty of time to get out."

"I was taking no chances," Bob nodded, rubbing his shoulder and grimacing. "I'm going to shoot first around here and argue afterward. Now where the hell is our party?"

"They scattered into the brush when the herd came down upon us," said Bright, glancing around for a sign of the men. "I haven't seen hide nor hair of one of 'em since. Perhaps they've returned to the *Annihilator*..."

CHAPTER FIVE
A New Danger

FEARING for their lives, Commander Allison and Lieutenant-Commander Bright remained for a long time beside the great tree in whose higher branches lay the still body of the monster reptile. Around them the prehistoric jungles roared with awe-inspiring life. But gradually the tumult subsided as the beasts slowly forgot about the strange sounds created by the invaders. Then the two officers of the *Annihilator* found themselves immersed in a dead silence. Cautiously they strode, side by side, pistols ready, toward the edge of the stagnant pool. The ground was mucky from the pounding of tremendous feet. The water lizard had vanished. A commotion in the center of the pool told them that other creatures were feeding upon the remains.

Then out of the oppressive silence came a sudden, prolonged shriek of the *Annihilator's* sirens. The two officers stiffened rigidly and regarded each other in blank amazement. Almost at once there came the muffled crack of staccato explosions, finally followed by the rolling boom of the ship's high-powered rifles. From which direction the sounds came, they could not determine. The roar and crash sounded solidly around them. Bright stared into the tightlipped features of his superior and addressed him.

"Sounds like a fight, Commander!" he gasped. "Maybe the *Annihilator* is being attacked by some creatures..."

"We'd better scout around and find out," exclaimed Bob. "Which way did we come to get down here?"

"I think we came down that bank on the other side," Bright replied, tensely. "We can follow the party's tracks back to the meadow…"

Whatever intentions or hopes Lieutenant-Commander Bright had of following the tracks of the party back to the *Annihilator* were immediately quashed when it was discovered that all boot-prints had been obliterated by the pound of animal feet. Not a human spoor remained to be observed! Frightened, maddened beasts had covered them completely, leaving not so much as a heel-mark anywhere in the muck that might direct the two officers in the direction of the *Annihilator*.

It was with the grim realization that they were lost and deserted that they started up the steep, mucky bank that they thought led to the land on which the *Annihilator* was grounded. But they fought their way up the slippery side of the slope and presently stood on a tree-covered plain. It was not the grassy meadow upon which the ship had settled, and while they stood there gaping at a huge dinosaur that stood among the trees not far away, they realized that they were lost indeed! Bob pulled up his pistol in line with the beast's head, but Bright held his arm.

"We're lost, Commander," he said. "Better save your ammunition."

Bob lowered his gun, nodded and jammed it into its holster. Then they studied the lay of the land around them and decided to return to the pool in hopes of finding some hidden tracks of the party.

Scarcely had they gone a dozen feet down the slippery incline when a stone-tipped spear thudded into the ground between them. They paused, amazed and bewildered, to watch the shaft vibrating like a fast-moving pendulum. Instantly they lunged for their pistols, studying the terrain below them.

What they saw on the other side of the pool caused them to recoil and crouch, horror-stricken!

Across the swamp a half-hundred blood-curdling creatures with scaly, human-like bodies and Triceratopsid* heads, stood on the fringe of the jungle and watched the crouching officers on the bank. They stood upright on two feet like a man, but their heads were the most frightful things Bob Allison or Bright had ever beheld. With a large bony armor curving down from the tops of their heads and across their shoulders, and savage, cruel eyes inserted above beastly snouts, the creatures sent stark terror surging through the two officers.

Then one of the beasts poised a spear and let it fly. It curved a graceful arc over Bob's head and buried its point notch-deep, in the soft earth. Mechanically he lifted his pistol and fired into the horde. The foremost Triceratopsian was torn to shreds as the missile from the gun exploded in his chest.

Instantly the space between the two humans hummed with singing darts. A barb scraped Bright's neck, creasing the flesh. He let out a stream of oaths and fired rapidly at the creatures below. He was an expert shot with a pistol and as rapidly as he could pull the trigger, his ears were rewarded by muffled explosions and terrible, beastly screams. But the Triceratopsians held their ground and hurled spear after spear in the direction of the death-spewing pistols.

* Referring to a giant plant-eating dinosaur.

Bob held his fire after his first shot, until Bright's pistol clicked on an empty cylinder; then he fired. Bright reloaded swiftly and by turns they sent missiles of terrible destruction into the horde in the swamp. Spears came from everywhere and then finally screaming arrows stirred up a hornets' nest of buzzing around them. An arrow went through Bob's visor like a bullet, lifting it back on his head; then another creased at his boot-top, glanced off, and lay beside him. He glanced at it quickly. The dart was tipped with an ivory head, sharpened to needlepoint and notched along the edges. It made him shiver and he turned again to the horde that seemed bent upon annihilating them.

Captured!

THE creatures were spreading out into a long line now, as though preparing to rush. They sent a stream of arrows at the two half-hidden humans, their huge bows twanging loudly, and then as by some signal, they broke and rushed. As they came, Bob and Bright retreated slowly up the bank, firing rapidly at the fast-running beings in an effort to check their rush. Arrows continued to sing around their heads, and they wondered at the miracle that kept them among the living.

Standing on the top of the incline they again paused.

A barrage of darts whistled past them and they decided that things were getting too hot for them. They turned abruptly and raced headlong toward the trees. The dinosaur had vanished, but weird forms scuttled under the branches.

The triceratopsians followed on the run. They were flanked by others now, which had come upon the scene

like glistening, scaly beasts of a nightmare. Bob Allison
and his first officer kept on steadily toward the trees. Small
animals scurried out of their path on stilted legs. They
were ant-like creatures as large as domesticated cats and
made strange noises as they ran.

Then as the two officers entered the fringe of the jungle,
they found themselves confronted by another battalion of
the grotesque creatures. From behind massive tree-trunks
surged a veritable army of Triceratopsians. They came
forward at once, spears upraised, and the two humans
discovered that they were now surrounded on all sides by
hideous, beastly beings who screeched triumphantly as they
closed upon them.

Standing back to back, Bob and Bright shot rapidly into
the ranks that slowly closed around them on all sides.
They sent slug after slug into them, mangling horribly
those who were hit. Bob hoped the others would become
frightened and retreat. But the Triceratopsians refused to
become frightened. Instead they fitted ivory-tipped arrows
into their powerful bows and let fly, but with mighty poor
accuracy.

Both men were nicked in a dozen places and blood
coursed down Bright's face from a crease across his scalp.
A sharp pain told Bob that an arrow had seared his thigh.
But he paid no attention to it. They fired as rapidly as they
could and by the time their pistols were empty, the horde
was upon them.

As he was being lifted bodily onto the broad back of a
frightful Triceratopsian, Bob brought his pistol down upon
the creature's bony head with a menace. There was a dull
thud and the creature merely snorted, while another yanked
the pistol from his hand. He received a sound cuffing
across the back from the fellow that had his gun, and then

lay still, panting and gasping for breath. He shot a quick glance toward Bright. The first officer lay on another broad back behind him, his face covered with blood and his head hanging grotesquely to one side.

"Bright!" Bob cried, apprehensively. "Bright!"

Lieutenant-Commander Bright's head moved slowly and wobbled drunkenly; then he managed to accumulate sufficient strength to raise it. Through blood-filled eyes he regarded the terror-stricken features of the commander and grinned strangely.

"I'm all right, sir," he said, faintly. "Guess I'm just weak from loss of blood!"

The creature who bore Allison turned his beastly head and looked at him. Bob recoiled from the awesome brute's breath, and squirmed to avoid it. Great hands, with three-taloned fingers and a cruel, bony thumb, clutched at him tightly and held him with a vise-like grip.

Bob shuddered and sucked in his breath.

The Triceratopsian that carried Bright paused and shook him like a rat in a terrier's teeth. Bright emitted a groan and lay still. His eyes closed and his head hung limply. Bob cursed under his breath as he saw the body of his officer go limp. Then he heard again the scream of the *Annihilator's* sirens, followed by a series of rapid explosions. To his ears finally came a deep-throated roar. He shrank against the broad back that carried him, well knowing what that roar meant. The *Annihilator* had suddenly taken to the air! Instinctively he searched the skies over his head. Far above him he caught the flash of a glistening body. From it trailed streaks of pale blue flame. Then it vanished like a will o' the wisp in the distance.

The *Annihilator* had deserted its commander and its first officer! Why it had suddenly taken off and roared out of sight Bob could not guess, unless it was because the ship too had been attacked by the Triceratopsians and was forced to flee for safety. But why had she gone beyond sight? He could not see or understand why such an impregnable craft as the *Annihilator II* would flee before a lot of old-world savages. But Bob Allison was destined to learn much of this old world before he became many days older...

A Mysterious Sound

FOR what seemed an hour, Bob lay across the back of the Triceratopsian that bore him through the jungle with little effort. Frequently he glanced at the inert form of Bright. Several times the first officer had groaned and Bob wondered if he was dying. Dry blood caked the man's features and the small area of skin that showed here and there on his cheeks was as white as death.

During all this time the creatures pushed through the jungle in an arrow-point formation. The bristling thickets with their sabre-like thorns did not hinder them, merely scraping against their scaled bodies and being brushed aside. But often strange thorns pricked the unprotected bodies of the officers, causing the flesh around the wounds to become dead for a time and then to pain nauseatingly. Their clothing was soon torn to shreds and they were suffering from head to foot.

They came upon another herd, this time one of imperial elephants, grazing in an open glade. They raised their trunks and trumpeted shrilly at the procession; then resumed feeding. The Triceratopsians seemed to have no fear of the huge beasts. They went right along as though they did not exist, and Bob wondered if the trumpeting was a kind of beastly salute.

After a period of precarious climbing, the Triceratopsians traversed a low range covered with vegetation and entered a wide, open valley. As they emerged from the jungle, Bob's eyes concentrated upon the burned hull of a huge airship. It lay in a twisted mass, beryllium girders and braces standing out like the bones of some grotesque skeleton. He studied the wreckage for a moment and then gasped. A thin plate of steel lay a few yards from the blackened frame. Upon it were the serial numbers and name of the lost explorers' ship, the *Skjangli!* He twisted his head toward Lieutenant-Commander Bright and yelled loudly.

"Bright!" he cried. "Snap out of it, old man! Look at that wreck!"

Bright managed to lift his head and to stare off to his right. His head wobbled and it must have been seconds before he could clear his brain of the stupor that clouded it. Then his eyes popped open with recognition.

"A wrecked airship!" he exclaimed. "It's not the—the *Annihilator,* is it?"

"You're goofy yet, Bright," said Bob. "Take a look at that steel plate laying in the open…"

Bright stared at the square of steel for a moment and then regarded his superior officer with flashing eyes.

"The *Skjangli!*" he snapped, hopefully. "The ship of the lost men…"

"Right," the commander agreed. "It's the *Skjangli,* the ship for which we've been searching."

Bright nodded.

"If the explorers were in some kind of a battle with these beastly devils," he said, "it's logical to think that the victors would burn or destroy the ship to prevent them from escaping."

"'Right you are," said Bob. "That's exactly what happened, I'll wager. Some powerful tribe annihilated the *Skjangli* and made off with the crew and passengers, even as they attempted to capture the *Annihilator*. Did you know, Bright, that the *Annihilator* has gone aloft and away—deserted us?"

Bright's mouth opened in a terrified expression. He stared at Commander Allison for a long moment and then groaned.

"Deserted us? In the name of heaven, how could they take off and leave us here to be slaughtered?"

"You must have been out then when she went away," said Allison, frankly. "I watched her disappear in the distance. But don't forget, old timer, that we're not dead yet, and the *Annihilator* will undoubtedly return…"

"I have scant respect for the young nincompoops in command of her now, Allison!" Bright swore, groaning and nursing his neck. His hand came away from the wound covered with clotted blood. He stared at it for an instant and then spat deliberately down the back of the beast that carried him. The Triceratopsian paid no heed to the insult, but merely went on without turning even his head.

The Triceratopsians had crossed the open ground and now headed again into the brush. Allison noticed well-worn trails on every hand now, and from far away, his ears detected the throb of drums. He decided that the sound must come from some tremendous kettledrums, for it was different from any other sound to which his ears were accustomed. The jungles were re-echoing the throbbing rumbles that sounded like steady, intermittent rolls of thunder, the beats timed to a second.

Bob relaxed his legs and arms and lay across the muscular shoulders of the brute, resigned now to whatever the future held for him. He watched the muscles play in powerful knots across the broad, scaled back of the Triceratopsian. From the neck down, the fellow was a fine specimen of human structure. But from the neck up, he was utterly loathsome.

Bob studied the creature's feet as it trod the trail. Its pedal extremities were clawed like its hands and spread out like the feet of some predatory bird. There were as many talon-tipped toes as there were fingers on his rather well shaped human-like hands. But the claws of each could have torn a man to shreds within a minute, so sharp and terrible were they.

The Triceratopsians were a head taller than Bob, making them close to seven feet high. They swung through the jungles with the ease and grace of an Iroquois, looking neither to the right nor left. They seemed to be the supreme rulers of all the beasts of the forests, and when any other creatures were encountered in the gloom-filled forest aisles, these either hissed, snorted or bellowed, and then resumed feeding. Everything, even the great savage mastodons and the towering dinosaurs, seemed to bow to the mysterious supremacy of this Triceratopsian horde, these strange beings, half-dinosaur and half-man.

Bob wondered at this great mystery, which, to him as a layman, was insolvable. He could hardly believe it possible for a modern man to be taken back into the dim ages of the beginning. The whole thing seemed like some wild nightmare and he wondered if he were really awake or dreaming!

But the swaying motion of the beast that carried him told him plainly that he was very much alive. And among other things, the persistent throb of thunderous drums informed him that they were getting nearer to the sounds. The thunder rolled down upon his ears more sharply now as though some giant creature stood before a mammoth drum and pounded it steadily with two mighty hammers, one in each hand.

Presently he found himself thinking of Joan. Would he ever see her again? Why hadn't he resigned his rank to carry out the plans for their marriage? What would she think when the world learned that the two commanders of the *Annihilator* had gone to their death at the hands of some terrible creatures deep within the earth? He doubted if the news would kill her, but it certainly would cast a shadow over the remainder of her life. He cursed himself for a fool for ever undertaking the venture in search of the lost scientists whose wrecked ship had already been discovered. Life certainly was cruel to him. Scarcely had he recovered from his experiences in the *Annihilator I* than he found his life imperiled again under even more frightful conditions. Disaster certainly hounded him...

CHAPTER SIX
The Beasts at Home

EVENTUALLY the procession went down a steep incline and entered upon another flat plain. The throb of the drums was very close now and Bob studied the terrain ahead. As far as his eyes could see there was a vast flat plain with towering lush grass swaying gently in a warm breeze. Great animals grazed here and there, their heads high above the waving grass. Two dinosaurs stood off to the left and regarded them for a long moment, then raced away like gigantic kangaroos. Every bound carried them entirely out of the grass and presently they vanished in the distance.

There was a sudden, terrifying scream from somewhere close at hand. Bob's hand went instinctively to his empty holster. The scream sounded like some giant in distress, so close was it. Then he caught sight of a great ground-sloth racing madly through the grass. A large, tawny cat, with tremendous fangs protruding from its jaws, tore after it, screaming the maniacal cry of the hunting jungle beast.

From his perch on the shoulders of the Triceratopsian he could watch the race of death as the animals appeared frequently in little open patches on the plain. The great sabre-toothed tiger was gaining rapidly. Presently it paused, crouched down in a little glade to bunch its muscles, and sprang into the air. There was a terrified squeal from the victim and then the lush grass at the spot was in terrific commotion.

For a few tense moments he watched the struggle and then all became still except for the gentle weaving of the grass under the influence of the breeze. The tiger had evidently won and had settled down to gorge.

Swiftly now the horde made headway. The creature almost ran along the wide, road-like trails before them. The Triceratopsian who carried Bob and Bright seemed tireless. They maintained the pace set by the others with little effort despite their burdens. Then suddenly the trail widened into a tremendous clearing in which stood innumerable mound-shaped dwellings of what looked like adobe mud. In the center towered one great structure above all others. It consumed an area of nearly an acre. The rest of the village was built around it in a circle, and Bob concluded, as a vast throng of Triceratopsians came forth to meet the procession, that the central structure was some kind of a council-house. He shot a quick, apprehensive glance at Bright.

The first officer of the *Annihilator* was sitting upright now upon the shoulders of his beast of burden. The Triceratopsian must have perched him astraddle of his neck so he could be carried more easily. Bright presented a strange sight, riding as though straddling a horse, on the neck of the grotesque beast, and Bob grinned. His friend seemed to be enjoying his ride now, for he had regained some of his lost strength and had managed to mop some of the clotted blood from his face. He was holding on to the creature, with his hands gripped on the curling plate of bone armor that ran from the top of his captor's head to shoulder level. His body swayed in rhythm with every quick step taken by the beast under him.

A tremendous crowd of Triceratopsians now stood in front of the procession. Half-grown Triceratopsian youngsters, grotesque little devils at best and filled with bloodlust, thronged the edge of the gathering, and picked up stones with eager hands. The mass broke suddenly and the procession entered an aisle packed on both sides by grunting, beastly creatures. Troops of youngsters fell in behind and Bob was forced to dodge small stones that were hurled at him by young hands.

Suddenly the two humans were placed on the hard-packed ground and shoved forward, side by side. The Triceratopsians fell in around them closely, as though to protect them from the barrage of stones that gleeful Triceratopsian brats were pelting them with.

"The dirty little rats!" snarled Bright. "I'd like to get my fingers on the throat of that leader...the biggest one of the mob. I'd certainly wring it for him!"

A small stone bounced off a Triceratopsian helmet and smacked Bob on the temple. His knees buckled under him from the numbing force of the missile and Bright held him up as a brute lifted a clawed foot to deliver him a sound kick for faltering. Bob groaned and shot a hand to his head. The force of the blow reeled him and a tiny stream of blood dribbled from his temple.

The Triceratopsians now strode so swiftly toward the great council-house that Bob and Bright, weak as they were, found it difficult to maintain the pace. Frequently the creatures behind them shoved them forward or delivered vicious kicks that at times almost sent them on their faces. Half running, they finally reached the huge structure and were picked up again in scaled arms. Then the procession entered and Bob and Bright were unceremoniously hurled upon what appeared to be an altar in the center of the large room.

A great gathering of Triceratopsians was already on hand, sitting in an unbroken circle around the altar like an audience in a circular theater. A few feet in front of the first row of leering spectators sat a tremendous brute. He towered head and shoulders above the others and held in his claw-like fists a knotted club that was stained with vermilion. Pendants of bone dangled from the shaft and a human skull hung suspended on a cord around his stubby, beastly neck.

Beside him squatted a white-haired human, his features half-hidden behind a stained, knotted beard, his eyes flashing with the same terrible cruelty that marked the apparent deviltry of the huge creature himself! The man was naked except for a narrow breechclout of tiger skin around his skinny, wrinkled loins. Around his waist was a cartridge bandolier and in a handy holster nestled an ancient pistol of the kind that had preceded the introduction of the modern guns that shot missiles filled with high explosives.

The Renegade

WHEN Bob's eyes fell upon the human who was evidently a white man well advanced in years, he was astonished beyond description. It was certainly strange to find a white man on intimate terms with the frightful beasts of this dawn-age jungle! And the man was sitting placidly beside a Triceratopsian who, to all appearances, was the chief of the horde. It was a mystery that caused both officers to stare incredulously at the man. How did he come to be there, and how did he manage to place himself so high in the esteem of the Triceratopsians as to give him a ranking position beside the cruel leader?

Bob and Bright sat up presently on the altar and stared around them. Evil faces confronted them on every hand. The throbbing of the drums smote upon their ears with a menace, then suddenly it ceased. For what seemed a long time they sat still, staring into the cruel features of the man beside the chief, as though too stupefied to speak.

The man regarded them calmly, never moving an inch. His eyes stared like the open eyes of the dead, never blinking. Had he been an image of stone, he could not have sat more still and rigid. He seemed to be trying to bore into the very souls of the two officers, and they shuddered. After a time Bob slowly pulled his pipe from a pocket, filled it with a fragrant tobacco from a small watertight container, and struck a match to it. Bright watched him through wide eyes as he held the match over the bowl and puffed. From out of the sides of his eyes Bob studied the creatures around him. Their mouths snapped open in astonishment when they beheld the match flame. The man beside the chief sat as immobile as a stone figure. Then Bob addressed him sternly.

"What's the big idea of taking us captive, old man?" he asked. "Have we harmed you or your vulgar friends in coming here?"

The ancient devil's tousled head moved a fraction of an inch, but his eyes bored straight ahead at the two ragged officers. Bob puffed on his pipe with a feigned calmness and wondered if the man understood English. Perhaps the man was dumb or long years spent with the awesome Triceratopsians had dulled his wits to any kind of human communication.

As he speculated upon the strange presence of the fellow in this remote world within the earth, he decided that he must be a lost polar explorer who had wandered across the open lake and entered the steaming jungles, over which he must now rule partly. He did not doubt that the man had lost all sense of respect for mankind. Men have been known to return to the jungle and cast all their civilized traits into the discard for the freedom of savagery.

"Well, can't you answer me?" Bob asked impatiently, putting on a bold front in an effort to bluff his way into liberty.

By the looks in the eyes of the Triceratopsians, he somehow felt that they held him in some kind of awe since he flicked his match into flame. He had read books of history in which men won freedom and safety by just such acts as striking a match at the right time, making their savage captors believe they possessed supernatural powers. That was the reason why he had lit his pipe when he did.

He blew a cloud of white smoke from his lips and spat deliberately at the feet of the squatting Triceratopsian ruler. The huge fellow blinked his eyes stupidly and stared at the two captives. Then the old man twisted his leathery lips into a snarl and spoke.

"Yes, I can answer you," he snapped. His voice seemed to come from between clenched teeth. "You have been taken into captivity by the Ruler of All who has forbidden the existence of humans in the world that cradled him. Our great chief, Hokar, master of the world within a world, makes war on all who trespass..."

"Then what the hell are you doing here?" Bright snapped heatedly. "You're a hell of a fine specimen of humanity to be in cahoots with a mob of cut-throats like this..."

"If I prefer the society of these people to your kind, it's none of your business," the man hissed with menacing evil.

"I chose these kind of beings rather than to continue living with your kind who drove me here!"

"Drove you here?" Bob asked incredulously. "What do you mean?"

Bright's eyes lighted with suspicion and he nodded at Bob.

"He's an escaped criminal who wandered north and found a way into the interior," he sneered, glancing furtively at the man to see the effect of his assertion. The man scowled and clenched his fists tightly.

"Exactly..." he growled tensely. "But you'll never get out to tell where I am."

"And why not?" Bob questioned, arching his brows in feigned surprise.

"Because it is the will of Hokar that you die even as others like you will die in the jaws of the Triceratops," the man snapped.

"Others?" gasped Bob, leaning forward. He had a vague suspicion of the true meaning of the man's words. Surely he did not refer to the lost explorers as the "others." Or had more of his own men from the *Annihilator* been taken?

"Others," the man repeated. "Swedes!"

"Then you *have* taken the scientists whose ship we saw wrecked on the way here?" asked Bob.

"Hokar has set the Swedes aside for his especial pleasure," the old man gritted as though he was trying to control a growing, insane anger that was burning within him for all humanity. "We wrecked their ship when it landed, and captured the lot to fill the belly of the sacred Triceratops..."

The Sentence

"GOOD Lord, man," said Bright savagely. "You couldn't stand aside and watch your kind murdered in cold blood…"

"Don't you fool yourself about me, mister!" he scowled, stroking his stained beard with a gnarled hand. "I've enjoyed it before and I'll enjoy it again when you two smart alecs go into the jaws of the beast which these good people worship as you worship your God…if you have one."

"You seem to forget that our ship, the *Annihilator,* will come back here and blow you all to hell," snapped Bob. "You might kill us, old man, but you'll die yourself as a result. My men will return here to demand our release. If you and Hokar fail, they'll blast the whole tribe to pieces."

"You can't frighten me or Hokar, young fellow," snapped the man with an evil hiss. "Its been tried before. You can't bull your way out. In the first place you killed a dozen of Hokar's men! He demands your lives in payment for them. And by hell you're going to pay his bill and mine too!"

"What's your bill?" quizzed Bob with sarcasm.

"Civilization has wronged me, young man…" Hokar's ancient lieutenant snarled. "It accused me of a murder that I did not commit! It confined me in your prison at Nome. It took my wife away from me…ruined me in the eyes of all men. They tortured me until trey made me confess to that crime; then sentenced me to hang! But I escaped. And all civilization is going to pay one of these days when Hokar's strength increases. He'll sweep the whole surface clean! But you're going to be the first on account. Your lives are going toward the settlement of civilization's debt

165

to me. It will be a pleasure to see two officers of the United States Air Forces die a dozen deaths in one!"

"You're crazy," grumbled Bright, amazed. "You're as crazy as a loon…"

"Who are you, anyhow?" gasped Bob, smiling grimly at the old fellow's evident insanity.

"You wouldn't know me," the man hissed. "I escaped from Nome before you were born. But if it'll do you any good…I am Richard Brandt, formerly of Seattle and Nome…"

"Never heard of you," said Bob. "What you did before you came here is nothing to me. We're not responsible for your hatred of society."

"Every civilized man is responsible!" growled Brandt.

He nudged the grotesque beast beside him and addressed him in grunting tones. Hokar bent close to him and snarled like an angry beast. The two officers condemned to die in the jaws of the sacred Triceratops were amazed that Richard Brandt could converse easily with Hokar in the ruler's grunting speech. They conversed like snarling dogs for a moment and then Brandt faced the captives again.

"Hokar has set your doom for tomorrow when the mists clear from the face of the Central Sun," Brandt interpreted with a pleased grin. "At that time a thousand warriors will return from the place where they attacked your ship. They will bring other prisoners to die with you. Warriors from all Hokar's outposts will be on hand to witness the sacrifice…"

Bob and Bright were stunned into immobility, unable to believe their ears. It was hard to realize that death loomed over them like a grim, menacing spectre; but there was no doubt that Hokar and Brandt meant to carry out their plans for their destruction on the morrow. But how did Brandt know that Hokar's warriors had made a successful raid on the *Annihilator's* scouting party? Undoubtedly they had attacked the ship and failed, but by Brandt's words, they must have taken the scouting party that had retreated into the jungle when the mastodon herd thundered down upon it at the swamp. The two officers did not know the real significance of the throbbing drums, the wireless system of the savage tribes of Hokar. Richard Brandt must have taught the terrible Triceratopsians many things since he arrived among them. Communication by thundering drums must have been one of those things.

CHAPTER SEVEN
Imprisoned!

COMMANDER ROBERT ALLISON and his first officer Bright were taken without further ceremony out of the great council-house and led away. Outside a great mob had gathered to await the reappearance of the two officers who to them must have been as grotesque in appearance as any of the Triceratopsians were to the men from the *Annihilator*. Again mobs of Triceratopsian youngsters, armed with stones and sharp sticks, flew at them with a hatred. Bob kicked angrily at a savage, half-grown beast that had attempted to bite him, sending the beast spinning. Instantly a Triceratopsian cuffed him cruelly for his defensive act and they were led between mud houses and finally halted in front of a square stockade.

The mob followed, growling and snarling among themselves like a pack of hunger-crazed wolves. But they stood away at a safe distance now as two Triceratopsian warriors swung open a great gate leading into the stockade, which comprised towering logs, sharpened to points at the top like an old-time frontier fort. The two officers felt that Brandt had had a hand in having the stockade erected, for it was different from any other type of Triceratopsian structure. It showed human thought and genius at first glance.

They were led into the "pen" rapidly. A dozen savages of Hokar's horde, followed by Brandt himself, escorted them to the far side of the stockade and proceeded at once to peg them out spread-eagle fashion to the rough wall. Knowing the uselessness of resistance, they meekly permitted themselves to be tied, hands and feet, with twisted fiber thongs that bit into their wrists with stinging pain. The Triceratopsians were certainly taking no chances on their breaking their bonds and escaping, for the bonds were drawn tight and knotted, almost shutting off the blood from their hands.

Brandt himself inspected the thongs and grunted with satisfaction. He stepped off and surveyed the doomed victims with an air of supreme contempt.

"That's the beginning of your end," he snapped, waving the Triceratopsians away with a flip of his grimy hand. "You'll hang there until Hokar is ready to feed you to his sacred beasts..."

"You'll suffer for this, you old stiff," snapped Bob hatefully. "If I could get my fingers on you I'd wring your scaly neck, you dirty...!"

Brandt pulled his open hand back over his head and sent it with stinging force into the commander's writhing features. He groaned and sagged under the blow for it had great power despite the man's advanced age.

"That's what I think of you, young fellow!" Brandt hissed. "I could tear you to shreds with my bare hands if I felt like it. But I'll get more satisfaction in seeing you chewed up in hunks..."

"You're a yellow rat, Brandt!" Bright swore in his face.

Hokar's human lieutenant drew back his fist again and held it. He grinned and let it fall, nodding.

"Yellow or not won't save you, mister," he growled. "Another word out of you and I'll turn those savage brats in the pen to muss you up."

"Yeah?" hissed Bright.

"Yeah!" snapped Brandt, emphatically, turning on his heel and walking toward the gate, which banged shut after he made his exit.

Bright, staring around the stockade, now gasped out loud at what he saw.

Pegged out against the wall on the far side were the sagging forms of other men, hanging limply to their wrist-thongs! Bright let out a curse and hissed at Bob. The commander was hanging almost inert from the effects of Brandt's savage blow, but he looked up at the voice of his first officer.

"We're not alone here, Allison!" cried Bright, excitedly. "Look over there…"

Bob peered into the shadowy gloom across the stockade and gasped.

"Men!" he exclaimed. "Why they must be the members of the Swedish polar expedition. Are they dead?"

"They look it, Commander," answered Bright. "No…by heavens, they're alive all right. They must have thought it best to play dead when we came in. Hey, over there!"

A man with a heavy black beard shook his head wildly and looked up. His eyes flashed like pools of fire in the gloom as they found the source of the voice that brought him out of a stupor. He stood suddenly rigid against the wall, tugged at his wrist bonds, and then stared across the stockade stupidly.

"What's wrong with you fellows?" Bright asked, pausing for a reply.

The bearded man shook his head dumbly and shrugged his powerful shoulders. Then he turned his head to the man next to him and hissed like a snake to call his attention. The fellow lifted his head and surveyed his neighbor with alarm. They conversed in an alien tongue for a moment and then the second man faced the distant wall of the stockade.

"My associate does not understand English," he said weakly. "We've been sleeping from exhaustion, I guess. What are you doing here?"

"The great Brandt has pegged us out for sacrifice," Bob volunteered. "Do you men belong to the Swedish polar expedition?"

"Brandt?" the man hissed. "The filthy murderer... Yes, we are all that remain of the expedition. What brought you into the interior?"

"The United States Government sent us out to look for you," Bob replied without hesitation. "And we were investigating a strange open lake on the surface when we came upon this world. I was in command of the *Annihilator II,* our ship. With Bright here, I set out with a scouting party to explore around. We got lost and were captured by Hokar's brutes."

"I'm sorry, truly sorry we were the cause of your predicament," the Swedish scientist said sadly. "We were twenty men strong when we landed to investigate this interior world. Hokar's savages attacked our ship and destroyed it, killing ten men outright! Where is your ship now?"

"Gone..." said Bright. "The brutes attacked it and the officers in charge took her up. We've no idea where the *Annihilator* is now, but we have a feeling that she'll come back for us."

"Come back?" the man asked hopefully.

"She'll come back all right," snapped Bob. "And when she does, Brandt and Hokar will see hell popping!"

Hopeless

By this time, ten weary men, standing rigid against the wall opposite the two officers, were all staring with wide-eyed wonder. Professor Donalsen seemed to be the only member of the bedraggled expedition who could speak English, and he acted as spokesman for his fellows. He talked the whole matter over with the *Annihilator's* commanders and explained to his comrades all that was said. Bob and Bright saw their eyes flashing with joy as they learned that the *Annihilator* had attempted to find them. But they were suddenly downcast when they were informed of the ship's take-off, leaving its chief officers stranded. Bright interrupted the scientist and regarded him curiously.

"When has Brandt timed you for death?" he asked bluntly.

"He hasn't set any time yet," the scientist replied gloomily, "but we expect it with each passing hour. He's just playing with us now...killing us with anxiety and apprehension. And you...?"

"When the mists clear from the face of the Central Sun," Bright growled. "When will that be?"

"That will be tomorrow by our reckoning," said the professor tensely. "Each night there is a mist before the sun, probably steam, and when it clears, Hokar's horde worships the Triceratops, a great beast to which they bear a striking resemblance. We've seen the beast! It is a tremendous creature of the reptilian class, with a head like the savages, and a squat body with a long, bone-studded tail. The Triceratops is to these creatures what the great ape is to our kind. Here man-like beings sprang from the animal Triceratopsids, as the humans sprang from the simians of our world, resulting in the creation of a Triceratopsian culture over which Hokar rules."

"Well, cheer up, we die in the jaws of the Triceratops when the mists clear tomorrow!" said Bright. "Unless the *Annihilator* shows up before that time, I guess our bones go to the Triceratopsian brats..."

Professor Donalsen shuddered and sucked in his breath.

"The Triceratops will leave no bones to be picked, friend," he said.

"Have you tried to get loose?" Bob asked suddenly. The scientist laughed harshly.

"Certainly, but it is futile. Brandt had Dr. Jorgenssen flogged for even trying. They watch us almost constantly, waiting like carrion for one of us to die..."

For the next few minutes the explorers talked among themselves. Bob hung his head resignedly with thoughts of Joan uppermost in his mind. Strangely he did not worry much about his own life. He dreaded more the shock she would suffer when he failed to return or if word was handed to her telling of his death. But that seemed unavoidable now. He must pay with his life for the apparent injustice of man-made laws and civilization against one man—whose broodings had created within him an insane hatred for all mankind.

CHAPTER EIGHT
Other Victims

THE sun in this strange interior world did not set like the sun of the Solar System. Instead it seemed to stand almost overhead now like a fixed star of the proportions of the moon as seen from the surface. A foggy mist was beginning to form an obscuring photosphere around it, not hiding it entirely, but causing the sphere to glow like a cold, clammy ball.

Days and nights here were determined by the clouds of mists that formed over the central sun with as unceasing regularity as our own solar sun slips down in the west to herald the approach of night, and rises again in the east with the dawn of a new day. And the disk looked as cold and chilly as an arctic moon, but Bob Allison felt no change in temperature when the central sun became almost hidden from his view by the mists.

Strangely, the climate did not vary, remaining as fixed as the interior sun itself. He watched the clouds for a time and then the ghostly shadows that danced around him on all sides with the fall of a deadly gloom over the domain of Hokar. Shadows were everywhere, lurking like evil spectres in the corners of the stockade. An interior night was at last on hand and the jungle seemed to awaken to it by creating a ceaseless din.

Those in the stockade shuddered when they heard the terrifying scream of a sabre-toothed tiger. Great mastodons were evidently crashing through the matted brush on all sides of Hokar's city of mud mounds. Huge insects droned overhead in swarms. Bat-like birds with membraned wings flapped dismally over the open stockade like great carrion. Some of them hesitated in their slow, deliberate flight, and circled the stockade. One flew very close, and Bob saw its eyes flashing like fire-flecked rubies as it surveyed the scene below.

Then suddenly Hokar's city went into pandemonium! Those within the stockade were terrified by the gutturals that came from innumerable Triceratopsian throats. The sounds harmonized with the beastly grunts, screams and groans that emanated in the jungles beyond the town, but they were now so close that the doomed humans were horrified. What was happening, anyhow? Was the *Annihilator* returning? Had it been spotted by the Triceratopsians, creating uncontrolled excitement among their horde? Allison would soon learn the reason for the excitement.

After a time, the stockade gates were swung open again and in marched a dozen humans guarded by a squad of Hokar's warriors. They were immediately pegged out against the wall adjacent to the two officers, and deserted. The gates crashed shut and presently the town became still again. Hokar's thousand warriors had returned from their raid on the *Annihilator* and they had brought with them what remained of the scouting party.

Instinctively Bob counted them as they were pegged out, keeping silent through the entire process. Then he heard the men swearing and cursing the hand of Fate that had led them into the claws of these brutes. Bob remained silent until after the gates closed; then, staring into the gloom, he addressed his men. Bright had been dozing and was too stupefied to make a sound.

"What happened, men?" tensely Bob asked. "Can you see me?"

He was aware that all heads had been turned in his direction and all eyes were staring at him. Then he heard the nearest man gasp excitedly.

"Commander Allison!" the man ejaculated, his voice filled with amazement.

"Yes, it's me," said Bob softly, peering at the shadowy forms.

"We thought you were killed when the herd of elephants stampeded, sir!" the man gasped. "Then under command of Lieutenant Backus we retreated back toward the *Annihilator*. But when we reached the meadow we found the ship was being attacked by the savages. They had somehow brought a great herd of huge mastodons into the fight and hurled them at the *Annihilator*. The animals would have wrecked her in no time with their heavy charging, and the ship took off for protection. We were captured after a fight. Lieutenant Backus and Professor Marble were speared. We left twenty-three dead on the ground…"

"Backus and Marble killed?" Lieutenant-Commander Bright interjected suddenly.

"Killed at the first skirmish. Dr. Ralston and Sergeant Ringer were so badly wounded that they were left on the ground to die. Ringer had an arrow through his chest and Ralston was run through by a spear."

"Yeah…" volunteered a man next in line. "And the devils drank the blood of the dead and left the dying to the carrion!"

"My God," groaned Bob, blanching. "That's terrible…"

"Terrible is right, sir," the man admitted. "But what's going to happen to us?"

"I—I don't know, men," Allison said dismally. "Lieutenant-Commander Bright and myself are condemned to die in a few hours. What's left of the Swedes are here, too, awaiting death. You'll probably follow…"

The men groaned. Every ear had heard and then from across the stockade came the brave voice of Professor Donalsen.

"If we could get loose, Commander Allison," he said in low tones, "there's enough of us to put up a good fight and go down like men…"

Bob tugged savagely at his bonds and felt them give just a trifle, but the fiber thongs bit into his flesh and held. He grunted with pain and gave it up.

"Good idea, professor," he gritted. "But get loose first. It can't be done!"

The Coming of Dawn

LONG before the mists vanished from around the central sun, Hokar's city was awake. The din of the jungles had subsided slowly after a time and, as an interior morning dawned, became altogether silent. The Triceratopsians seemed to have worked themselves into a beastly silent frenzy during the gloomy night and had reached the climax as the shadows gradually lifted from the town.

They made terrifying sounds now outside the stockade and the pounding of countless feet on the hard-packed earth around the council-house told those within the pen that they were stamping a savage ritual. It seemed that their number had increased three-fold during the night, and now the mounded city was in an uproar.

The humans, pegged out for slaughter or sacrifice, had spent a terrible night. Every time Bob's eyes closed in sleep, he was rudely awakened by the bite of the thongs into his wrists as he sagged inert. After a while he gave up all thought of rest and contented himself with standing erect. Bright swore for hours to relieve his mind and stood awake beside his superior officer.

Gradually the mists cleared from the central sun and it began to glow like a ball of red fire, causing steam to rise from the jungles in clouds, dissolving slowly in the atmosphere, which reeked with decaying carrion and other terrible smells of the town. All night Bob had watched the space overhead for a glimpse of the *Annihilator II,* hoping the hope of a doomed man that she would heave into view and rescue them. But the *Annihilator* seemed to have deserted the interior world entirely for she did not appear.

Then presently the stockade gates swung open and a dozen Triceratopsian warriors swung rapidly in. They went at once to the two officers, whom they cuffed cruelly with raking claws, before releasing them from the stockade. The warriors then closed around them in an impenetrable circle and marched them out of the pen.

As they went, Bob glanced toward his men. They were fighting at their bonds, trying to get loose. Groaning and swearing, they hurled vile epithets at the grotesque fighters of Hokar's tribe. The Triceratopsians paid no attention to them. As they passed the Swedish scientists, the unfortunate men began to yell loudly in protest. The cries were taken up by the American flyers, and the stockade was in a sudden bedlam.

But the Triceratopsians looked neither to right nor to left. They went about their business like mechanical men, carrying out the will of some superior mastermind.

A great throng of savages was on hand to greet the victims with hostile sneers, snarling grunts and savage gutturals. To Bob and Bright it seemed that the whole jungle had suddenly become on friendly terms with one another and had congregated to watch the annihilation of the condemned strangers. A wide aisle was made in the crowd and the two officers were led through it past the great council-house to what appeared to be a tremendous amphitheater on the edge of the town.

In the center of a depression stood a huge, barred cage, and in it was a huge, terrifying beast with a head like the savages of Hokar's band and the body of some great, scaly lizard!

Bob shuddered when he beheld the thing. Saliva, as red as blood, dribbled from its mouth, and when it caught the scent of the two humans, it lowered its great head and grunted thunderously, pawing the earth like a maddened bull. The sacred Triceratops was ready to pounce upon the two officers and devour them like flies in the jaws of a dog!

As they strode swiftly toward the cage, Bright suddenly faltered. Two giant Triceratopsians grasped him by the arms and hustled him forward. A vicious kick sent him sprawling on his face. Bob rushed forward and picked him up. Bright was blubbering like a frightened infant. His nerve had snapped and hurled him on the verge of insanity. But Bob kept cool. For no nameable reason, he had a hunch that the Triceratops was going to be cheated. During the past few moments his hopes had been strangely lifted from the depths. He faced the situation with a grin, looking upon it as an adventure from which he would be snatched when the jaws of death yawned open for him.

"Buck up, Bright," he said. "Cripes! A man only dies once, and it'll all be over in a minute. Stick out your chest, old man, and think about the *Annihilator* coming..."

179

"I've given up all hope, Allison," Bright moaned. "I'll go completely crazy in another minute. I'm not ready to die… I've got a family…kids and all, back in Kitty Hawk. What'll become of them when I'm gone?"

"Don't worry about that," Bob soothed. "Uncle Sam always takes care of the families of its men. They'll be provided for."

Bright broke down now and wept. Bob placed an arm around his shoulder and held him up. The first officer was on the verge of complete collapse. He could have died with a grin in a fight, but facing such a terrifying beast as the Triceratops, whose jaws bellowed for his flesh, was something else again and his nerve quit him.

Within twenty feet of the cage the procession halted. From the side came Hokar, followed by Brandt and a double line of Triceratopsian priests. Hokar was adorned in a flowing robe of feathers making him look like some strutting bird with the head of a beast. Brandt was likewise adorned and he grinned evilly as he quick-stepped to the side of the chief. In their rear, the grotesque priests, each carrying a skull-crowned scepter and painted hideously in red streaks, maintained a grunting chant that rose and fell with a two-toned menace.

Then the drums began to throb in the village. They increased in volume until the plain thundered. The rumble smote upon the officer's ears like the steady crash of high explosives. Bob held his hands over his ears for a moment's relief. Bright ignored the sounds as though lost in his own terrified emotions. As a result of Bob's urging, he banished his tears and finally faced death like an officer and a man, stiff and rigid, calm and aloof.

Hokar paused in front of them. Brandt leered and the priests circled in crescent formation behind them. Bob heard a sudden high-sounding hiss and looked up mechanically. It sounded like the drone of the *Annihilator's* exhausts. But the space over his head was fathomless and empty. Brandt laughed loudly at the move and then scowled.

"You needn't hope for your ship to return, dog!" he said. "She's gone—scared away. I'm told she quit this world entirely and returned to your filthy civilization…"

Bob glowered at him for an instant and then deliberately spat in his face. Brandt sprang forward at once, jerking at the ancient pistol that dangled at his belt. But free from bonds as he now was, Bob quickly stepped forward and hurled his right fist with all his strength at the renegade's writhing features. It collided with Brandt's temple and sent him sprawling. Allison would have been shot on the spot for his act had not Hokar placed a clawed hand on Brandt's shoulder and shoved him off balance. An iron slug from his hand-made cartridges whined past Bob's ear and thudded into the broad, scaly chest of a warrior behind him. The Triceratopsian grunted and wilted. He got up, stared about him stupidly and vanished in the crowd that had followed.

Hokar emitted a few guttural snarlings at his lieutenant and then knelt down before the two officers. He scraped his bony head on the ground, snarling like a wolf. The priests continued their chanting and Hokar stood erect. Brandt rose and scowled menacingly, but made no further attempts to cheat the Triceratops.

Wreaths of damp club-mosses were placed on the officers' heads by two priests. This ceremony was followed by a guttural incantation, and the savage ritual was ended. Hokar bowed again and slowly strode away. Brandt bent over in mock reverence and hurried after the chief. They took up a position on the edge of the amphitheater depression and stood majestically surrounded by the priests. Bob and Bright were led closer to the cage by four warriors. Around the saucer surged the population of the town and the visitors who had come in during the night.

Two Triceratopsians went to the cage and pulled out the lock-peg. The door swung open of its own weight as the warriors raced away to the safety of higher ground. Bob and Bright were left standing alone before the open cage. The Triceratops pawed the earth and came crawling into the open, head lowered, eyes glaring, and blood dripping from its mouth. Then the beast charged like an express train, straight toward the horrified officers!

CHAPTER NINE
The Annihilator Comes!

TOO horror-stricken to move, Bob and Bright stood rooted to the ground and stared at the oncoming beast. The ground under their feet seemed to throb under the weight of the Triceratops. Then, suddenly realizing that death was almost upon them, Bob gave Bright a powerful shove out of the brute's path, and then leapt aside himself. As he did so, he heard disappointed grunts from the numerous Triceratopsians standing on the higher ground, who were watching with the lust for blood. But Allison paid little attention to them now. He was fighting to keep away from the giant creature...the idol of this prehistoric world.

Scarcely had he stepped aside than the Triceratops thundered past. As it went it lashed out with its thorny tail and droned over Bob's head with a scant few inches to spare. Bright picked himself up from the ground, stared around him, and began to run. The Triceratops spun around like lightning, bellowed once and pursued him. Waving his arms wildly to distract the attention of the maddened beast from the running first officer, Bob saw Bright dash around the cage and reappear on the opposite side. The Triceratops was almost upon him. Then—an unexpected thing happened.

With scarcely ten feet to go before closing its great jaws around Bright, the Triceratops was seen to falter suddenly to its fore-knees. Instantly there was a muffled explosion and the brute's head appeared to explode in bloody fragments! Its tail lashing madly through the air, its body jerking in violent convulsions, the Triceratops lay headless upon the ground.

Dazed, Bob stared at it for an instant and then raced toward Bright. They came together and crouched.

"Someone's shot the brute!" Bob cried.

"Look...we're saved!" shouted Bright, looking up. High overhead was a long, silvery body, glistening like a needle, in the glare of the sun. *"The Annihilator!"*

Bob glanced upward.

The *Annihilator* was circling high above and coming closer with each passing second. The ship was dropping down over the domain of Hokar, a single stream of flame roaring like a waterfall from her tail exhausts.

Shut in on all sides by a ring of Triceratopsians, Bob and Bright glared around them for some avenue of escape. They expected the savages to swoop down upon them at any instant to claw them to shreds. But the beasts seemed too stupefied at the sudden death of their monstrous idol to act. They stared upon the scene dumbly, and then Bob heard Brandt's high-pitched voice urging them into the depression.

As he looked around him, Bob suddenly realized that the explosive projectile that had killed the Triceratops had not come from the high-flying *Annihilator*. The ship had been too high for such accuracy; the missile had come from a pistol! Someone armed with a regulation government pistol was in the neighborhood to protect them from the jaws of the beast—who could it be? Certainly none of the men inside the stockade were armed; and they couldn't have shot the beast even if they had been, because Allison had left them trussed against the walls and there was no way to escape from their bonds. Besides, all pistols and rifles had already been taken by the Triceratopsians.

Hardly had the mystery of the beast's death entered his mind than six rapid-fire explosions sounded in back of him. They both swung around instantly in the direction of Hokar and his priests.

Hokar, his body having been torn to shreds, lay upon the ground in an inert, bloody heap! It was a ghastly sight. And around him lay the motionless bodies of five of his priests. Brandt stood like a stone image beside his fallen leader, mouth agape, astonished. The sudden turn of events appeared to have stunned him. Then pandemonium overcame the crowd. The whole horde broke into savage cries of fright and raced back toward the town.

Overhead, the *Annihilator* floated majestically. From her aerial torpedo tubes, arranged just under her airfoils, shot a sudden stream of black cylinders. Bob watched them race earthward. He was violently hurled flat on his face when the first of the torpedoes exploded in the midst of the running horde.

"They'll blow the hell out of the stockade, Bright!" Bob shouted, lying on his stomach a dozen feet from the beheaded Triceratops.

"Can't be helped if they do, Commander," said Bright, breathing heavily as he spoke. "But I don't think they'll hit it, because the observers have probably spotted those of us within…"

Some strange instinct warned Bob Allison of approaching disaster to his rear. The peculiar sense that tells men that they are being watched or stalked, told him that danger still lurked near him despite the fact that the whole Triceratopsian horde was apparently in terrorized flight. He rolled over on his back suddenly and leaped erect.

The Man in Disguise

BRANDT, his eyes flashing with an evil, deadly light, was advancing cautiously toward him, pistol in hand and ready to fire...

With a sinking sensation down in the pit of his stomach, Bob crouched instinctively. Bright sucked in his breath and sat up, his face suddenly pale. Brandt laughed like an insane creature and flipped his pistol in line with Bob's head.

"I'm going to drop you, young fellow," he snapped, "then plug your mate. I'm not going to be cheated. You'll pay—you'll both pay! I've prepared for just such a thing as an air raid. Your ship can't touch me. Are you ready to take it between the eyes now?"

"Don't be a fool, Brandt!" said Bob excitedly. "Lay off and you'll be pardoned by the government. We can straighten out your case..."

"No, you can't," Brandt growled, bestially. "I wouldn't take a pardon even if you could do it. I quit your civilization years ago and I'm still quits. Hear me? Now down on your knees..."

"Can't you listen to reason, Brandt?" Bob appealed futilely. The man was undoubtedly crazy and would kill him in cold blood despite his pleading.

Brandt cackled like an idiot and then scowled.

"Down on your knees, young feller!" he hissed again. "Down so I can watch you grovel at my feet!"

"You can go to hell then!" Bob snapped, bunching his muscles to spring at the insane convict. "I grovel at no man's feet!"

He heard the ancient pistol's mechanism click as the hammer was being drawn back. A shudder surged through his body as be lurched forward like a cornered beast. Brandt's pistol roared loudly in his face. He felt a sharp pain shooting through his shoulder and a black nausea clutching at his brain. But he fought to keep his faculties and groped blindly for the whiskered throat in front of him.

Blinded by a screen of red, savage under the influence of an uncontrollable anger, Bob Allison heard the pistol roar again and then his fingers encountered a grizzled throat. With all the strength at his command, be closed them tightly into the yielding throat of his insane enemy.

Brandt brought his gun down upon Bob's shoulder with terrific force. Bob felt the strength fleeing from his fingers. The pistol fell again and his hands came away from that savage throat. He heard Brandt chuckling as he fell and cringed to stay the shock of an expected bullet. He closed his eyes and groaned; then suddenly came a muffled explosion. He felt something wet and heavy strike him in the face. Bright yelled and he opened his eyes.

What he beheld caused him a horrible nausea. Brandt's ancient body lay in mangled bloody tatters in front of him. An explosive missile had blown him to pieces. Sick, his senses swimming, Bob rose and wiped his face. His hands came away bloodstained. Striding swiftly toward them from the opposite side of the depression was the figure of a Triceratopsian. He held a pistol in a human hand and it was smoking!

Awed and wholly uncomprehending, Bob and Bright watched the approaching figure, amazed at the white hands that protruded strangely from underneath a scaled cloak. Then as the thing approached they saw him shove the pistol into a cartridge belt and literally tug at his head.

They saw the head of a Triceratopsian torn from scaled shoulders and before them stood the grinning form of Sergeant Ringer!

"Ringer!" Bob and Bright gasped together.

"At your service, sirs!" said Sergeant Ringer, saluting.

"What in hell's the idea, Sergeant?" Bob exploded with a ring of joy in his voice. "We were told you had been left wounded back on the meadow…"

"I was wounded, sir," Ringer said, slipping out of the skin of a Triceratopsian warrior and casting it aside with a look of loathing. "But not so bad as the devils thought. An arrow punctured me on the chest, causing a lot of blood to spill but doing little damage. But Ralston died shortly after the savages left us."

"Sergeant," said Bob extending his bloodstained hand, "you'll be cited and promoted for this, sir. How did you do it?"

Sergeant Ringer blushed under smears of Triceratopsian blood and stood at attention.

"Just an old trick, sir," he said. "I played the role of wolf in sheep's clothing. When the devils left the meadow, I skinned one of their dead and draped it around me to make me look like one of them. Then I trailed 'em through the jungle to the town. I hid all night in a hole not far from here and waited my chance to get among them without creating suspicion. After they took you from the stockade I slipped in and turned the other men loose. They told me you were to be sacrificed and I just happened to get here in time to shoot the animal as it bore down upon Mr. Bright. To scare the lot I blasted the big fellow over there, and then watched the old man when he stalked you. I held my fire, thinking you'd want to settle with him yourself, until he got the top hand, and then I let him have it, sir."

"You're a very brave man, Sergeant," said Bright. "A very brave man, indeed. Sergeant, I salute you, sir!"

Lieutenant-Commander Bright stood suddenly at attention and lifted his right hand in a stiff salute. Sergeant Ringer blushed and returned it.

"Where are the men from the stockade?" Bob inquired, grinning; his hands trembling.

"They're concentrated on the edge of the town, sir, just within the jungle," said Ringer. "Some of them are armed, for I brought three pistols with me. They're safe, providing the *Annihilator* doesn't plant a torpedo among them..."

Overhead the *Annihilator* hovered like a tremendous bird and spread death into the Triceratopsian town. The world inside of the Earth trembled with each deafening explosion of aerial torpedoes. Then after a time the huge craft dropped lower and the three men, safe in the depression, heard the rattle of machine gunfire. The ship's guns hissed and rattled, sending explosive messengers of death into the Triceratopsians who, without a leader, went mad with fright.

A savage raced down into the amphitheater suddenly to escape the deadly fire from the *Annihilator*. Sergeant Ringer lifted his pistol and sent him to death without hesitation. Eventually the three climbed to higher ground to survey the damage.

Hokar's horde was broken; his town lay in devastation. Great holes yawned like craters in it where the powerful torpedoes had exploded. Bloody masses lay on every side. The *Annihilator* had done her work well. Hokar would never increase his strength for a raid on the civilized world! His savage warriors were almost exterminated, even as he himself had been killed instantaneously by Sergeant Ringer's deadly pistol.

The *Annihilator* had played her part for mankind in preventing some future catastrophe. She had played her role, unconscious of the fact that she was wiping out mankind's most terrible enemies. But she had not performed without losses. Thirty-five of her men lay dead on the meadow.

After the *Annihilator* had landed in the center of the devastation she had wrought, she took on the lost Swedish explorers, the two officers and the remainder of the ill-fated scouting party. Then she went at once to the meadow, where a party was landed to bury the remains that were left after the savage beasts of the jungle had gorged. The *Annihilator II* planted an American flag above them and proclaimed the world on the interior as a possession of the United States of America. And who could deny her right to it after she had conquered it? Certainly the Swedish explorers made no objection.

After a brief ceremony, over which Bob Allison officiated, the *Annihilator II* set her course for the surface and eventually emerged under the brilliant rays of the arctic sun. She streaked across above the fields of ice, in a straight course for Markham Island, where the two radio-television men were picked up. She ultimately reached Kitty Hawk, where every man was hailed as a hero.

But in Joan's eyes Commander Bob Allison was the greatest of them an, and a great celebration took place throughout the nation when the two were joined in marriage by the chaplain at Kitty Hawk.

THE END

If you've enjoyed this book, you will not want to miss these terrific titles…

ARMCHAIR SCI-FI, FANTASY, & HORROR DOUBLE NOVELS, $12.95 each

ARMCHAIR SCIENCE FICTION CLASSICS, $12.95 each

ARMCHAIR MASTERS OF SCIENCE FICTION SERIES, $16.95 each

If you've enjoyed this book, you will not want to miss these terrific titles…

If you've enjoyed this book, you will not want to miss these terrific titles...

ARMCHAIR SCI-FI, FANTASY, & HORROR DOUBLE NOVELS, $12.95 each

D-21   **EMPIRE OF EVIL** by Robert Arnette
THE SIGN OF THE TIGER by Alan E. Nourse & J. A. Meyer

D-22   **OPERATION SQUARE PEG** by Frank Belknap Long
ENCHANTRESS OF VENUS by Leigh Brackett

D-23   **THE LIFE WATCH** by Lester del Rey
CREATURES OF THE ABYSS by Murray Leinster

D-24   **LEGION OF LAZARUS** by Edmond Hamilton
STAR HUNTER by Andre Norton

D-25   **EMPIRE OF WOMEN** by John Fletcher
ONE OF OUR CITIES IS MISSING by Irving Cox

D-26   **THE WRONG SIDE OF PARADISE** by Raymond F. Jones
THE INVOLUNTARY IMMORTALS by Rog Phillips

D-27   **EARTH QUARTER** by Damon Knight
ENVOY TO NEW WORLDS by Keith Laumer

D-28   **SLAVES TO THE METAL HORDE** by Milton Lesser
HUNTERS OUT OF TIME by Joseph E. Kelleam

D-29   **RX JUPITER SAVE US** by Ward Moore
BEWARE THE USURPERS by Geoff St. Reynard

D-30   **SECRET OF THE SERPENT** by Don Wilcox
CRUSADE ACROSS THE VOID by Dwight V. Swain

ARMCHAIR SCIENCE FICTION CLASSICS, $12.95 each

C-7   **THE SHAVER MYSTERY, Book One**
by Richard S. Shaver

C-8   **THE SHAVER MYSTERY, Book Two**
by Richard S. Shaver

C-9   **MURDER IN SPACE**
by David V. Reed

ARMCHAIR MASTERS OF SCIENCE FICTION SERIES, $16.95 each

M-3   **MASTERS OF SCIENCE FICTION, Vol. Three**
Robert Sheckley, "The Perfect Woman" and other tales

M-4   **MASTERS OF SCIENCE FICTION, Vol. Four**
Mack Reynolds, Part One, "Stowaway" and other tales

If you've enjoyed this book, you will not want to miss these terrific titles…

ARMCHAIR SCI-FI & HORROR DOUBLE NOVELS, $12.95 each

D-31   **A HOAX IN TIME** by Keith Laumer
        INSIDE EARTH by Poul Anderson

D-32   **TERROR STATION** by Dwight V. Swain
        THE WEAPON FROM ETERNITY by Dwight V. Swain

D-33   **THE SHIP FROM INFINITY** by Edmond Hamilton
        TAKEOFF by C. M. Kornbluth

D-34   **THE METAL DOOM** by David H. Keller
        TWELVE TIMES ZERO by Howard Browne

D-35   **HUNTERS OUT OF SPACE** by Joseph Kelleam
        INVASION FROM THE DEEP by Paul W. Fairman,

D-36   **THE BEES OF DEATH** by Robert Moore Williams
        A PLAGUE OF PYTHONS by Frederik Pohl

D-37   **THE LORDS OF QUARMALL** by Fritz Leiber and Harry Fischer
        BEACON TO ELSEWHERE by James H. Schmitz

D-38   **BEYOND PLUTO** by John S. Campbell
        ARTERY OF FIRE by Thomas N. Scortia

D-39   **SPECIAL DELIVERY** by Kris Neville
        NO TIME FOR TOFFEE by Charles F. Meyers

D-40   **JUNGLE IN THE SKY** by Milton Lesser
        RECALLED TO LIFE by Robert Silverberg

ARMCHAIR SCIENCE FICTION CLASSICS, $12.95 each

C-10   **MARS IS MY DESTINATION**
        by Frank Belknap Long

C-11   **SPACE PLAGUE**
        by George O. Smith

C-12   **SO SHALL YE REAP**
        by Rog Phillips

ARMCHAIR SCIENCE FICTION & HORROR GEMS SERIES, $12.95 each

G-3   **SCIENCE FICTION GEMS, Vol. Two**
        James Blish and others

G-4   **HORROR GEMS, Vol. Two**
        Joseph Payne Brennan and others

If you've enjoyed this book, you will not want to miss these terrific titles…

ARMCHAIR SCI-FI, FANTASY, & HORROR DOUBLE NOVELS, $12.95 each

D-41 **FULL CYCLE** by Clifford D. Simak
IT WAS THE DAY OF THE ROBOT by Frank Belknap Long

D-42 **THIS CROWDED EARTH** by Robert Bloch
REIGN OF THE TELEPUPPETS by Daniel Galouye

D-43 **THE CRISPIN AFFAIR** by Jack Sharkey
THE RED HELL OF JUPITER by Paul Ernst

D-44 **PLANET OF DREAD** by Dwight V. Swain
WE THE MACHINE by Gerald Vance

D-45 **THE STAR HUNTER** by Edmond Hamilton
THE ALIEN by Raymond F. Jones

D-46 **WORLD OF IF** by Rog Phillips
SLAVE RAIDERS FROM MERCURY by Don Wilcox

D-47 **THE ULTIMATE PERIL** by Robert Abernathy
PLANET OF SHAME by Bruce Elliot

D-48 **THE FLYING EYES** by J. Hunter Holly
SOME FABULOUS YONDER by Phillip Jose Farmer

D-49 **THE COSMIC BUNGLERS** by Geoff St. Reynard
THE BUTTONED SKY by Geoff St. Reynard

D-50 **TYRANTS OF TIME** by Milton Lesser
PARIAH PLANET by Murray Leinster

ARMCHAIR SCIENCE FICTION CLASSICS, $12.95 each

C-13 **SUNKEN WORLD**
by Stanton A. Coblentz

C-14 **THE LAST VIAL**
by Sam McClatchie, M. D.

C-15 **WE WHO SURVIVED (THE FIFTH ICE AGE)**
by Sterling Noel

ARMCHAIR MASTERS OF SCIENCE FICTION SERIES, $16.95 each

MS-5 **MASTERS OF SCIENCE FICTION, Vol. Five**
Winston K. Marks—Test Colony and other tales

MS-6 **MASTERS OF SCIENCE FICTION, Vol. Six**
Fritz Leiber—Deadly Moon and other tales

If you've enjoyed this book, you will not want to miss these terrific titles…

ARMCHAIR SCI-FI & HORROR DOUBLE NOVELS, $12.95 each

D-51   **A GOD NAMED SMITH** by Henry Slesar
         WORLDS OF THE IMPERIUM by Keith Laumer

D-52   **CRAIG'S BOOK** by Don Wilcox
         EDGE OF THE KNIFE by H. Beam Piper

D-53   **THE SHINING CITY** by Rena M. Vale
         THE RED PLANET by Russ Winterbotham

D-54   **THE MAN WHO LIVED TWICE** by Rog Phillips
         VALLEY OF THE CROEN by Lee Tarbell

D-55   **OPERATION DISASTER** by Milton Lesser
         LAND OF THE DAMNED by Berkeley Livingston

D-56   **CAPTIVE OF THE CENTAURIANESS** by Poul Anderson
         A PRINCESS OF MARS by Edgar Rice Burroughs

D-57   **THE NON-STATISTICAL MAN** by Raymond F. Jones
         MISSION FROM MARS by Rick Conroy

D-58   **INTRUDERS FROM THE STARS** by Ross Rocklynne
         FLIGHT OF THE STARLING by Chester S. Geier

D-59   **COSMIC SABOTEUR** by Frank M. Robinson
         LOOK TO THE STARS by Willard Hawkins

D-60   **THE MOON IS HELL!** by John W. Campbell, Jr.
         THE GREEN WORLD by Hal Clement

ARMCHAIR SCIENCE FICTION CLASSICS, $12.95 each

C-16   **THE SHAVER MYSTERY, Book Three**
         by Richard S. Shaver

C-17   **THE PLANET STRAPPERS**
         by Raymond Z. Gallun

C-18   **THE FOURTH "R"**
         by George O. Smith

ARMCHAIR SCIENCE FICTION & HORROR GEMS SERIES, $12.95 each

G-5   **SCIENCE FICTION GEMS, Vol. Three**
        C. M. Kornbluth and others

G-6   **HORROR GEMS, Vol. Three**
        August Derleth and others

If you've enjoyed this book, you will not want to miss these terrific titles…

ARMCHAIR SCI-FI & HORROR DOUBLE NOVELS, $12.95 each

D-61   **THE MAN WHO STOPPED AT NOTHING** by Paul W. Fairman
TEN FROM INFINITY by Ivar Jorgensen

D-62   **WORLDS WITHIN** by Rog Phillips
THE SLAVE by C.M. Kornbluth

D-63   **SECRET OF THE BLACK PLANET** by Milton Lesser
THE OUTCASTS OF SOLAR III by Emmett McDowell

D-64   **WEB OF THE WORLDS** by Harry Harrison and Katherine MacLean
RULE GOLDEN by Damon Knight

D-65   **TEN TO THE STARS** by Raymond Z. Gallun
THE CONQUERORS by David H. Keller, M. D.

D-66   **THE HORDE FROM INFINITY** by Dwight V. Swain
THE DAY THE EARTH FROZE by Gerald Hatch

D-67   **THE WAR OF THE WORLDS** by H. G. Wells
THE TIME MACHINE by H. G. Wells

D-68   **STARCOMBERS** by Edmond Hamilton
THE YEAR WHEN STARDUST FELL by Raymond F. Jones

D-69   **HOCUS-POCUS UNIVERSE** by Jack Williamson
QUEEN OF THE PANTHER WORLD by Berkeley Livingston

D-70   **BATTERING RAMS OF SPACE** by Don Wilcox
DOOMSDAY WING by George H. Smith

ARMCHAIR SCIENCE FICTION & FANTASY CLASSICS, $12.95 each

C-19   **EMPIRE OF JEGGA**
by David V. Reed

C-20   **THE TOMORROW PEOPLE**
by Judith Merril

C-21   **THE MAN FROM YESTERDAY**
by Howard Browne as by Lee Francis

C-22   **THE TIME TRADERS**
by Andre Norton

C-23   **ISLANDS OF SPACE**
by John W. Campbell

C-24   **THE GALAXY PRIMES**
by E. E. "Doc" Smith

If you've enjoyed this book, you will not want to miss these terrific titles…

ARMCHAIR SCI-FI & HORROR DOUBLE NOVELS, $12.95 each

D-71   **THE DEEP END** by Gregory Luce
       TO WATCH BY NIGHT by Robert Moore Williams

D-72   **SWORDSMAN OF LOST TERRA** by Poul Anderson
       PLANET OF GHOSTS by David V. Reed

D-73   **MOON OF BATTLE** by J. J. Allerton
       THE MUTANT WEAPON by Murray Leinster

D-74   **OLD SPACEMEN NEVER DIE!** John Jakes
       RETURN TO EARTH by Bryan Berry

D-75   **THE THING FROM UNDERNEATH** by Milton Lesser
       OPERATION INTERSTELLAR by George O. Smith

D-76   **THE BURNING WORLD** by Algis Budrys
       FOREVER IS TOO LONG by Chester S. Geier

D-77   **THE COSMIC JUNKMAN** by Rog Phillips
       THE ULTIMATE WEAPON by John W. Campbell

D-78   **THE TIES OF EARTH** by James H. Schmitz
       CUE FOR QUIET by Thomas L. Sherred

D-79   **SECRET OF THE MARTIANS** by Paul W. Fairman
       THE VARIABLE MAN by Philip K. Dick

D-80   **THE GREEN GIRL** by Jack Williamson
       THE ROBOT PERIL by Don Wilcox

ARMCHAIR SCIENCE FICTION CLASSICS, $12.95 each

C-25   **THE STAR KINGS**
       by Edmond Hamilton

C-26   **NOT IN SOLITUDE**
       by Kenneth Gantz

C-32   **PROMETHEUS II**
       by S. J. Byrne

ARMCHAIR SCIENCE FICTION & HORROR GEMS SERIES, $12.95 each

G-7   **SCIENCE FICTION GEMS, Vol. Four**
       Jack Sharkey and others

G-8   **HORROR GEMS, Vol. Four**
       Seabury Quinn and others

If you've enjoyed this book, you will not want to miss these terrific titles…

ARMCHAIR SCI-FI, FANTASY, & HORROR DOUBLE NOVELS, $12.95 each

D-81   **THE LAST PLEA** by Robert Bloch
THE STATUS CIVILIZATION by Robert Sheckley

D-82   **WOMAN FROM ANOTHER PLANET** by Frank Belknap Long
HOMECALLING by Judith Merril

D-83   **WHEN TWO WORLDS MEET** by Robert Moore Williams
THE MAN WHO HAD NO BRAINS by Jeff Sutton

D-84   **THE SPECTRE OF SUICIDE SWAMP** by E. K. Jarvis
IT'S MAGIC, YOU DOPE! by Jack Sharkey

D-85   **THE STARSHIP FROM SIRIUS** by Rog Phillips
FINAL WEAPON by Everett Cole

D-86   **TREASURE ON THUNDER MOON** by Edmond Hamilton
TRAIL OF THE ASTROGAR by Henry Haase

D-87   **THE VENUS ENIGMA** by Joe Gibson
THE WOMAN IN SKIN 13 by Paul W. Fairman

D-88   **THE MAD ROBOT** by William P. McGivern
THE RUNNING MAN by J. Holly Hunter

D-89   **VENGEANCE OF KYVOR** by Randall Garrett
AT THE EARTH'S CORE by Edgar Rice Burroughs

D-90   **DWELLERS OF THE DEEP** by Don Wilcox
NIGHT OF THE LONG KNIVES by Fritz Leiber

ARMCHAIR SCIENCE FICTION CLASSICS, $12.95 each

C-28   **THE MAN FROM TOMORROW**
by Stanton A. Coblentz

C-29   **THE GREEN MAN OF GRAYPEC**
by Festus Pragnell

C-30   **THE SHAVER MYSTERY, Book Four**
by Richard S. Shaver

ARMCHAIR MASTERS OF SCIENCE FICTION SERIES, $16.95 each

MS-7   **MASTERS OF SCIENCE FICTION AND FANTASY, Vol. Seven**
Lester del Rey, "The Band Played On" and other tales

MS-8   **MASTERS OF SCIENCE FICTION, Vol. Eight**
Milton Lesser, "'A' as in Android" and other tales